BEAUTY WITH
A BOMB

m. c. grant

A Dixie Flynn Mystery

BEAUTY WITH A BOMB

MIDNIGHT INK
WOODBURY, MINNESOTA

First Edition
First Printing, 2014

Book design and format by Donna Burch-Brown
Cover design by Ellen Lawson
Cover Image: 83318617/© Mitchell Funk/Photographer's Choice/Getty Images
Editing by Nicole Nugent

Midnight Ink, an imprint of Llewellyn Worldwide Ltd.

Library of Congress Cataloging-in-Publication Data
Grant, M. C., 1963–
  Beauty with a Bomb / by M.C. Grant. — First edition.
    pages cm. — (A Dixie Flynn mystery)
  ISBN 978-0-7387-3983-0 (alk. paper)
1. Women journalists—Fiction. 2. Human trafficking—Fiction. 3. San Francisco (Calif.)—Fiction. 4. Mystery fiction. I. Title.
  PS3607.R362953B43 2014
  813'.6—dc23
                              2014015162

Midnight Ink
Llewellyn Worldwide Ltd.
2143 Wooddale Drive
Woodbury, MN 55125-2989
www.midnightinkbooks.com

Printed in the United States of America

DEDICATION

To Karen and Kailey,
who fill my life
with passion, kindness, and love.

ONE

Heavily pregnant, the woman stands on the precipice of the parking garage. Her hands are raw from gripping the steel barrier, her legs nearly blue from the cold Pacific wind that lifts her woolen skirt and nips at her flesh.

Six stories below, a crowd gathers. The audience is a quivering mass of gaping mouths and wide, excited eyes—none quite believing what they're witnessing and yet none daring to look away.

A shimmering halo appears above each head as the rising sun reflects off glossy smartphones—everyone racing their neighbor to be first to YouTube the moment, to share their shock with the world in exchange for a high hit-count and a slice of Google ad revenue.

Uniformed police erect a barrier to keep the curious away from the splatter zone, just in case efforts to talk the woman off the ledge fail.

And they will.

Ania Zajak has had enough of words and false promises—especially those spoken by men. In all her nineteen years, she has never met a decent one; never felt a touch that wasn't followed by a sting; never known passion, kindness, or love.

She believed things would be different in America—a new life, a fresh start. She had wanted to be young, to wear patterned stockings and a scandalously short skirt, meet a nice man with kind eyes, and discover what it meant to laugh.

Ania had seen them laugh, the American women on TV. It was never the rich ones with their fake beauty and empty lives; all they managed to do was complain about unimportant things. The women who laughed the most were the ones who looked more like her—plain and ordinary, easily overlooked in a crowd.

And yet when those women laughed, a light burned so brightly in their eyes it was as though their very souls were dancing there. Ania had tried to copy them, but she never saw the light dance in her own eyes. She knew that was because imitation was not the same as the real thing. She had wanted to find someone who could show her what true laughter was, but the men she met wore cruel smiles that made their eyes darken and proved their souls had been replaced by poison and puss.

Ania strokes her swollen belly, wishing she could rip open the skin and scoop her insides out. But what good would that do? If she survived, some brute would simply force it full again and send her on her way.

There is no escape. Not for her.

There never was.

———

"Miss?" Detective Sergeant Frank Fury moves cautiously toward the woman. She is wearing a heavy, patterned shawl around her shoulders that drapes down over her engorged stomach, but it's still not enough to cut the wind and keep her warm. "You asked to talk with me?"

Ania turns to face him, the small movement making her sway off balance, and she momentarily loses her footing before refastening her grip on the rail. The crowd below gasps in unison and more twinkles appear.

He stops dead in his tracks and holds up his hands. "Please," he says. "Be careful. We don't want to lose you."

Ania smiles. It is one of the nicest things anyone has ever said to her. *We don't want to lose you.*

Pity that she is already lost.

"You are police detective named Frank?" Ania asks.

She has a heavy accent, yet her pronunciation of each word is near perfect. At one time, she must have had a good teacher. Frank can't quite pinpoint the origin, however. It's not Russian, thank God. He's had his fill of those vicious brutes lately—but somewhere close to that Baltic part of the world.

"I am," Frank answers.

"You are older than I imagine you to be."

"Sorry to disappoint."

"No," says Ania. "Not disappoint … only observation."

"Well, what do you say we observe somewhere warmer? If you move away from that ledge, we can grab a coffee and Danish downstairs. I know a—"

"That will not be happening, Frank," Ania interrupts. "Sorry. I know you are doing job, but this is not happy day with happy end."

Frank swallows and tries to calculate the distance between him and the woman. He's no longer built for speed, but if he can edge a little closer—

"Please," says Ania. "I like your eyes more when they are not this."

"Not this?" Frank asks.

"*Podejrzliwy*. Like a cop. They turn to steel, and I have had too much of steel. I like it better before when you show worry about me. Were you sincere?"

Frank uncoils and gazes at her. "I was. I am."

She smiles. "Do you have *dzieci*, Frank?"

Frank's brow furrows in puzzlement.

"Apology," says the woman. "Sometimes the proper word is stuck in my head, but my tongue is already moving, impatient to speak. *Dzieci* is children. Do you have children, Frank?"

He moves his head in the negative.

"Pity. Kind men should have many children to make up for every bastard who ruins a young life."

Frank clears his throat, uncomfortable with the personal nature of the conversation. "Why did you ask to see me?"

"It's not you I need."

"Oh? But—"

"I read the newspapers. You are friends with the reporter, Dixie Flynn. Is true?"

Frank bristles slightly and his lips tighten. "I know Dixie."

Ania reads his face. "You are not friends?"

Frank glances over his shoulder at the cops who are standing far-ther back before answering. "Yeah, we're friends," he admits. "Just had a bit of a disagreement recently."

He can almost hear the on-call counselor who's eavesdropping on their conversation cursing his not-in-the-official-handbook hon-esty. Plus, the Beagle-faced civilian was already upset that Frank, a Homicide detective with a reputation for kicking down doors rather than negotiation, was brought in to replace him at the bequest of the suicidal woman.

"You should forgive her, Frank," says Ania. "I read her stories and imagine she is, how you say, impulsive … Like a race horse without a rider, yet still with blinders, no? She needs her friends. You both do."

Frank's mouth twitches. "Interesting observation."

"Does she laugh?"

"Loud and often and usually when it's most inappropriate."

Ania smiles wider. "That gladdens my heart."

"Why all the questions about Dixie?"

"I need to see her."

"If you climb back over that barrier, we can—"

"No!" Ania interrupts. "The barrier protects us both. I told you this would not be happy day. I want to see her here, in person, be-fore I go. I know you can make this happen."

"If I don't?"

"Then I fall now."

Ania releases one hand from the railing and her body twists against the unforgiving wind and the cruel pull of gravity. Her knees and thighs tremble from fatigue, and her dark chestnut eyes speak volumes. This is not a bluff.

"Please," says Frank. "I'll get her."

"Be quick, Frank. I grow tired."

"Just hold on. We can make this better."

Ania returns her free hand to the rail. That is the second-nicest thing anyone has ever said to her. Pity it has to be today, her final one.

———

Twenty minutes later, Frank meets Dixie at the top of the stairs leading to the roof of the multistory parking garage in the heart of downtown San Francisco.

Dixie looks as if she has just rolled out of bed and redressed in the same clothes from the night before that were discarded in a heap on the floor. Her jeans have rips above each knee that were more likely earned through some careless act of mischief than purchased off a designer's rack, while her overwashed purple T-shirt is sprinkled with orange cat hair and a splotch of melted chocolate that appears to have been partially licked.

Her green leather trench coat with the awkward zipper down the back has lost more of its luster as a wet cloth has recently attempted to remove a multitude of stains from mud to blood and who knows what else. And in true, ladylike fashion, she's wearing her battle-worn biker boots.

Frank doesn't ask, but he assumes she's also slipped her pearl-handled switchblade into the moleskin pocket of her right boot.

Of course, this is also how she normally looks—not just when she's awakened pre-breakfast by the police. Not one for makeup or spending time in front of a mirror, Dixie is a take-it-as-you-see-it kinda gal.

At the top of the stairs, Dixie greets him with large, emerald eyes. She tries for a butter-wouldn't-melt coolness to her expression, but her whites are webbed with red veins either from lack of sleep, too much booze, or (more likely) a combination of both.

"It's been awhile, Frank," she says.

Frank exhales heavily. "We'll talk later, but I have a pregnant woman standing on the edge of this building with every intention of jumping. The only thing stopping her is you. She wants to talk."

"Why me?" Dixie asks.

"Ask her," says Frank. "But tread carefully. She's not bluffing."

———

Ania watches Dixie approach. Like the detective, she is older than expected. Not by much, but a few extra lines show upon the freckled map of her heart-shaped face. Still, Ania thinks she is an understated beauty with eyes hot enough to melt iron. Her ginger hair is an unkempt flame, while her clothes are a mess of contradictions. She is the writer, focused too internally to notice what her exterior is saying.

"That is close enough," says Ania.

Dixie stops moving, but she looks uncomfortable out in the open, as though unsure if she should smile or show concern. In what must be unusual for her, she is having trouble finding the right thing to say.

"My name is Ania Zajak," says Ania, breaking the ice.

"What's the accent?"

"I am Polish."

Dixie makes an unguarded face. "I never did understand borscht. Beet soup, really? It looks as bad as it tastes."

Ania feels a pleasant bubble form in her stomach that rises to her lips and breaks upon a smile. "You should have tasted *matka*'s. I never knew a meal was supposed to have flavor until I came to America. I like your Big Mac."

Dixie smirks. "If you want to try a real burger, I'll take you to Pink Bicycle. Best in the city."

Ania's smile fades as she releases the railing with one hand, shakes the cramps out of her fingers, and then touches her belly.

"How old are you?" Dixie asks.

"Nineteen."

"I remember that age. And if I were you, I'd get off that ledge right now because life gets so much better once you're out of your teens."

"Not for me."

"You'd be surprised. But let me guess: stupid prick of a boyfriend, stupider prick of a dad, and a mom who doesn't know when it's time to stand up for her daughter. How'd I do?"

Ania shakes her head and opens the shawl to expose a red plaid shirt with fake pearl snaps. The shirt is unflattering; not something a woman chooses to wear, but Ania does so only because it's large enough to fit.

Grabbing a lapel with one hand, Ania snaps open her shirt to expose an ill-fitting beige bra and her bloated stomach. The stretched skin looks near translucent and ready to pop, while a vivid red cesarean scar runs a few inches below her belly button like a madman's grin. The fresh wound is being held together by thick, black thread.

"You have other children?" Dixie asks, clearly confused.

Ania shakes her head.

"But the scar?"

"Is one of many."

Dixie's eyes lift from the woman's stomach to meet her focused gaze. Her verbal defenses lowered, her voice has lost its protective edge. "What can I do?"

"I need you to tell my story."

"I will. Let's get down from here. Go for breakfast and you can tell me everything."

"I would like that."

Dixie holds out her hand and takes a tentative step forward. "All you have to do is take my hand."

"It is too late."

"No, Ania, it's not. How can I tell your story unless you talk to me?"

"You will find a way."

"I can't. Not without you."

"No." Ania smiles. "You are smarter than that. A cookie, right? Tell my story."

"I will, but—"

With a simple, almost imperceptible slide of her feet, Ania's heels drop over the edge. In the same instant, her hands release their grip on the rail.

Ania's body falls backward as Dixie screams.

TWO

DIVING FOR THE RAILING, my outstretched hands skim a flutter of fabric, but there is nothing substantial to grab on to. I feel Frank's strong hands clutch my shoulders as we both watch the woman fall. Her eyes are closed, her lips mumbling a prayer—and then, before she hits the ground, she explodes.

I hear my own screams again as the woman's body evaporates in a bloody mist and fleshy chunks rain down on the mortified crowd of onlookers. The heat and energy of the blast sends me and Frank spilling backward onto the ground, ears ringing from the noise, mouths agape.

I try to put the horror into words, but the only sound that escapes my throat is a wail of despair.

Frank reaches for my hand and squeezes. "I have no idea," he says in response to the unspoken question. "But I'll find out."

"You won't be the only one."

I pull myself into a sitting position and stare over at Frank in complete disbelief. His face is reflecting the same confused agony of mine—except, let's face it, he's far uglier.

Dixie's Tips #19: *In times of stress, always go for humor over tears. A grim joke cuts through the shock before paralysis can lock your muscles into whimpering rigidity. And, if nothing else, it lets you know you're still alive. The dead are a humorless lot.*

The uniformed officers sweep past us to lean over the edge and gape at the carnage below. The slack-jowled counselor rushes to join them but takes the time to slow down for a moment and flash me an angry and disapproving scowl—just enough to make me feel even worse.

He wouldn't be so damn cocky if he knew that instead of tears, my usual response to emotional distress is to kick someone in the balls.

The moment he reaches the edge and looks over, the counselor turns back, his face suddenly green. Instead of veering off to one side where there is an entire rooftop of empty space, he bends double and vomits where he stands.

Frank growls at the sight before furrowing his brow and taking charge.

"Is anyone on the street injured?" He has to yell, as a hundred car alarms in the parking levels below us are blowing their electronic rape whistles at full, ear-damaging volume.

The uniformed officers, wide-eyed and dumb with shock, stare back at the burly detective sergeant, who is still sitting on the ground yet radiates a commanding presence that towers above them.

"Use your radios," barks Frank. "Get me a report. We'll need the bomb squad, forensics, paramedics, fire department, and the coroner." He stabs a finger at each officer in turn and instructs him or her exactly what duty to perform. "And somebody shut off these bloody alarms."

With his officers occupied, Frank slowly rises to his feet. His face contorts in pain and he grits his teeth to muffle a series of moans, groans, creaks, and pops. When he's erect, he holds out a hand to pull me up beside him.

"You OK?" I ask.

"Old bones," he grumbles.

We both absently brush dust off our clothes, taking a moment to gather our thoughts and slip into our professional armor: Frank has his gun, badge, and a mug that says he's a bastard with a short fuse; I have a notepad, daring haircut, and a razor-sharp tongue that can cut anyone's masculinity down to an embarrassing size.

I reach over and use my thumb to wipe a splash of blood from his cheek. He digs out an old-fashioned, white cotton handkerchief from his pocket and hands it to me.

"You need more than a thumb."

I wince. "Thanks."

"In all my years …" Frank pauses and I watch him struggle to control the emotion in his voice, not wanting to display any drop of weakness in front of the younger patrolmen.

"Her name is Ania Zajak," I tell him, taking control, yelling to be heard over the alarms. "She was nineteen and Polish."

Frank swallows and hardens his eyes. "We'll run a check. See if she has any next of kin in the country."

A uniformed officer approaches, his eyes shifting from Frank to me as though unsure if he should speak in front of a reporter.

"Spit it out," snaps Frank.

"We're getting reports of minor injuries from the street," says the officer. "Mostly cuts and bruises from people being knocked over. Several store windows shattered and injured people inside. Lacerations mostly, but nothing critical. A lot of people are suffering shock from being sprayed in blood and worse. The blast radius must have covered half the block. All departments are responding as ordered, so we should have the area locked down shortly."

"Get the fire department to block off both ends of the street," orders Frank. "I want officers taking statements and gathering contact info from everyone. Get the geek squad down here to collect video footage from cellphones and surveillance cameras, and then move the uninjured out before it becomes a bigger zoo. And get to work on those alarms. Call a locksmith and disconnect every car battery if you have to."

After dismissing the officer, Frank returns to the edge of the building and peers down. I follow and do the same.

We study the blood spatter, but its reach is immeasurable. Finding any part of Ania that's large enough for the coroner to examine is going to be problematic.

"She was always going to jump," says Frank as though reading my thoughts. "I saw it in her eyes."

"I felt I was getting through to her. She was so young. I just needed more time."

Frank squeezes my shoulder. His hand is like a baseball mitt, heavy yet reassuring. "There's nothing you could have done, Dix. She had already committed to this action."

"But why?"

Frank doesn't answer as he stares deeper into the chaos, his gaze taking in every inch

"What are you thinking?" I ask as his eyes narrow in concentration.

"Bottom line? My hands are tied. Homeland Security and the FBI will be all over this before the blood dries. This is the Boston Marathon all over again. It screams *terrorist.*"

"But?" I press.

Frank's mouth is a crooked twist of lips on a mug only his friends can love. "No shrapnel."

I raise an eyebrow. "Go on."

"Typically," Frank explains, "suicide terrorists wear a vest that's laced with steel ball bearings or nails to create maximum carnage. It's not the blast that kills most of their targets, but the shrapnel." He points toward the shattered store and office windows. "Each shard of glass becomes a knife, so imagine what a few hundred ball bearings would do."

"She wasn't wearing a vest. I think the explosives were"—I find it difficult to say the words—"inside her."

Frank grimaces. "That's a warped kind of evil."

"Except, I don't think she was. Evil, I mean."

Frank studies me with hard eyes.

"She didn't want to hurt anyone," I continue. "That's why she came up here. That's why she detonated before she hit the ground. She wanted to avoid killing people."

"No." Frank shakes off my suggestion. "She wanted us to witness this. It's a warning of more shit to come. She wanted us afraid. She wanted the entire city afraid."

"If that was her goal," I argue, "she would have asked for a TV reporter, not print."

Frank stabs his trigger finger down at the crowd and all the twinkling lights.

"Who needs TV?" he says. "Video of this is already screaming around the entire planet. If one person missed it, ten others didn't. By the time the media gets it on the air, it's already old news."

"Then why ask for me?"

Frank shrugs. "That's your puzzle; I'm waist-deep in my own." With a heavy sigh, he turns his back on the bloody scene and yells, "Is somebody working on these goddamn car alarms?"

———

When I walk into the newsroom of *San Francisco NOW*, the alternative newsweekly that is smart enough to employ me, six pairs of eyes widen and one junior reporter gasps.

I glance over my shoulder to make sure I've not accidentally allowed a horde of flesh-eating zombies to follow me up the two flights of stairs before asking, "What?"

"Your face," says one of the reporters.

"Ha ha," I mock dryly. "At least mine doesn't match my ass."

"No, really," continues the reporter, blushing slightly at the jab. "Your face is covered in blood."

"Oh." I remember Frank's handkerchief, but I had failed to use it. No wonder the taxi driver gave me the silent treatment. "It's OK. It's not mine."

I detour into the staff washroom and begin filling one of the sinks with warm water. Stripping off my coat, I study my T-shirt and decide it could use a spot treatment, too. After pulling it off, I look in the mirror and nearly gasp.

Above a sun-shy chest so pale that I often wonder if my skin contains any pigment at all, a thousand crimson freckles spatter my face and neck.

Jesus. I think of Ania's tortured face: youth, beauty, and a lifetime of sadness in those chestnut eyes. Who had done that to her? Who had stolen every last ounce of hope?

The door creaks open behind me.

"Dix. You OK?"

It's Lulu, the librarian in charge of the paper's morgue, where we keep all our dead stories and photos, and one of the few people who isn't afraid to challenge me when I'm being a moody bitch.

"Fine," I answer. "The blood's not mine."

I splash warm water over my face and scrub.

"You know," Lulu chuckles as she enters and closes the door behind her, "that doesn't exactly make me feel any better. Did you bludgeon somebody on the way to work? A construction worker whistle at your ass and you decided to deflate his pucker?"

"Not exactly." I look in the mirror again, catch where I've missed a few spots and dunk my face back into the water to scrub harder.

When I emerge, Lulu hands me several sheets of paper towel. "Were you at the bombing?"

I dry my face.

"She was only nineteen," I say.

"Who? The bomber?"

I nod.

"How do you know?"

"I talked to her ... before ..."

"Before she blew herself up?"

I nod again.

"Jesus, Dixie. You were that close?"

"She asked to talk to me before she jumped."

"Why?"

"To write her story, but before we even ... she just stepped off the ledge. One minute she was there, talking ... normal, you know? The next ... gone."

Lulu clucks in sympathetic understanding. "If I was ever going to do something that crazy, you'd be the one I wanted to write my story, too."

"Why?" I ask, digging to make sense of it all.

"Because you don't take things at face value. Every media outlet will be branding this girl a terrorist, but I can see it in your face already: you need to know more, you need to know why. Those other guys are satisfied with the headline and pictures. That's enough to instill fear and make people buy the next day's issue. But you're never satisfied with anything but the full story."

"She was Polish," I say quietly.

"And?" Lulu presses.

"When was the last time you heard of a Polish terrorist?"

Lulu grins. "See."

I drop the used paper towels into the trash and reach for my T-shirt. I pause at the sight of my reflection again: pale, freckled skin and white cotton bra. It's not my favorite article of clothing, and something I often prefer to go without. There's nothing fancy about it, no lace or silk, it simply does the job—not that my bosom gives it much of a workout. Ania's ill-fitting bra, however, looked like it had been handed down from someone who knew absolutely nothing about the garment. The cups were at least one size too small and the band was so tight it was practically crushing her ribs. It would have been achingly uncomfortable.

I turn my T-shirt inside out and slip it over my head. The stains will need more than a sponge bath with hand soap and paper towel.

Ready to face the world again, I turn to my friend. A big-boned woman with big hair, big boobs, and big hands, Lulu is still new to being a complete woman and as such dresses as flamboyantly as she did as a drag queen. Fortunately, she has the saucy attitude—and the legs—to get away with it.

"Can you dig up whatever stories we've run in the last six months on Polish immigrants or any recent violence or anomalies within the Polish community?"

Lulu grins again. "My pleasure."

———

In the newsroom, Stoogan is sitting at my desk—waiting. A grossly obese man with skin that is incredulously paler than my own, Edward Stoogan has the mind of a Pulitzer Prize–winning journalist trapped inside the body of a beached beluga whale.

An albino with shock-white hair, Stoogan's eyesight is so bad that his computer monitor is set up to display every story in headline-sized type, yet somehow he can spot my ginger hair anywhere in the newsroom.

"The answer is yes," I say as I approach.

"And what's the question?" he asks warily.

"Does this chair make my ass look big?"

Not even a snicker, but I can see by the glint in his rabbit-pink eyes that he's actually delighted to see me. Then again, I do have an overly active imagination.

"You were at the bombing," he says in a high-pitched squeak that makes him far too easy to impersonate.

I nod.

"I need a firsthand account ASAP to go on the web. We can link it to the public's YouTube videos. This thing is going viral and we need to be on top of it."

"Is that what we do now?" I ask. "Chase the dailies?"

Stoogan sighs. "Publisher wants us to be more proactive with the website. Get the stories up fast—"

"And check the facts later?" I interrupt.

Stoogan's cheeks go even whiter. "No, we still do our jobs."

"Except we're an alt-weekly for a reason. We make sure we do it right, ask the questions nobody else does, and give our readers the full story. We don't shoot from the hip and see what trash flies out."

Stoogan stands up and wipes a bead of perspiration from his upper lip. He's clearly in no mood to argue, which is odd.

Dixie's Tips #20: *Journalists are a cantankerous lot who will argue the color of snow if they've run out of politicians to bash. When they're holding their tongues or being overly nice, that's when you have to worry.*

"New mandate, straight from the top. You can still go in-depth for the print edition, you know I'll back you on that, but I need your online story on my desk in twenty minutes. Is that clear?"

"Yes, boss."

As Stoogan shuffles away, I resist the urge to make a snarky comment. As far as editors go, Stoogan is one of the best I've ever had. Pity the new publisher is pushing him too hard to generate revenue rather than good journalism. Do that long enough and eventually all you'll do is break your best people in half.

I toss my coat on the desk, switch on the computer, and pull the keyboard onto my lap. I don't have a lot of facts, but what I do have is likely more than anybody else.

I write what I know but leave one important detail out. Like an ace up my sleeve, I don't like to show the competition all my cards.

THREE

After filing the story, I head home to shower and change. In the lobby of the three-story Painted Lady that has been converted into six cozy one-bedroom apartments, I notice my mailbox appears unusually full.

Inside, the box is stuffed with at least two days' worth of unsolicited junk mail, a few unwanted bills, and two small packages wrapped in dark paper the color of blood.

The first package is slightly smaller than a paperback book, while the second is tall and relatively skinny, like a box for a fancy pen or a pair of custom chopsticks. My name and address is scrawled on the front of both in barely legible handwriting; the postal stamp is marked San Francisco, but there's no return address.

The last time I received a surprise gift, it turned out to be a kick-ass handgun—a Smith & Wesson Governor—from Frank. I wonder if these mystery parcels might be an apology from Pinch, a former hit man who recently strained our friendship when he unexpectedly came out of retirement.

Presents, however, especially if they're handguns or chocolate, are always a good way to speed up the healing process.

I carry the packages upstairs to the second floor and as I unlock the door to my apartment, I notice a small red ball resting on the ground.

I bend to pick it up. It's soft and spongy and roughly the same color as the two packages.

Inside, I immediately roll the ball across the hardwood floor and watch Prince Marmalade, my guard kitten and only boyfriend at present, spring awake to give chase.

With Prince busy tormenting the round intruder, I drop the mail on the kitchen counter, throw my soiled clothes in the sadly overflowing laundry hamper and head for the shower.

I make the temperature extra hot as I scrub every last trace of Ania's blood from my hair and body.

By the time I turn off the nozzle, the bathroom is clogged with steam and my skin is a vibrant pink. I wipe the excess moisture from my face and pull back the shower curtain just as a human shape emerges through the translucent cloud.

I scream. And so does the shape. It's high and girly.

"What are you doing, Dix?" Kristy yells. "I just about peed myself."

"I'm in my shower!" I yell back. "What are you doing?"

"I saw you come home." Through the fading mist, Kristy holds out a cup of coffee. "Thought you could use this."

Kristy lives directly across the hall with her girlfriend Sam, but there are times when I wonder why we even have separate doors as she'll find any excuse to barge through mine—especially when I forget to use the new deadbolts I had installed recently.

I accept the coffee and take a long sip. It's dark and strong—just the way I like it.

"My beans?" I ask.

Kristy grins. "I made it here. We're all out."

It's impossible to stay angry at Kristy, her heart is just too big.

"Thanks, but next time, wait until I'm out of the shower."

Kristy giggles and skips out of the room, giving me a few moments of privacy to towel off.

After dressing in fresh clothes with nary a bloodstain in sight, I join Kristy in the kitchen.

"You've got presents," she says, studying the red packages. "Who are they from?"

"I don't know."

"A secret admirer?"

"Or a clever bill collector."

"Open them. Biggest one first."

I unwrap the first package. Inside is a rectangular block of wood, painted bright red, with the letter D inserted into one of five slots in the front.

"That's weird," says Kristy. "Is there a note?"

I turn the paper inside out and examine the underside of the block of wood, but there's nothing.

"Try the next one," Kristy urges.

I open the second package. It contains a small red pole and the letter I. I insert the letter into the slot beside the D, leaving three blank slots still to be filled. The pole fits into a notch closer to the rear of the block.

"You know what that reminds me of?" Kristy says, wrinkling her nose.

"Hangman," I say.

"That's creepy, especially with DI on it. Who sent it?"

I check the packages again, but there are no notes. The blood-like color, however, fills me with unease.

Pinch's return to freelance murder was part of a bargain he struck with local Bratva chief Krasnyi Lebed, aka the Red Swan, to leave me alone. But who's to say a Russian gangster will keep his word?

A visible shudder runs down my spine.

"You OK, Dix?" Kristy asks.

"Yeah, I just need to get back to work. We'll talk later, OK?"

Kristy nods and skips to the door, but just before leaving, she turns. "Oh, by the way, we've got a new neighbor." She points to the ceiling above my head at the apartment once occupied by Derek and Shahnaz until they became uncomfortable living directly above me. The bullet hole in my ceiling (their floor) was the final straw. They moved across the hall and now live in the apartment above Kristy and Sam, which in my mind is a far more perilous situation. "I think he might be single, but he's got a lot of suitcases."

"Did you meet him?"

"Just a glance. Cute butt for a guy, though."

I grin. That's Kristy.

———

Before leaving the apartment, I call Lulu at the paper's morgue.

"Anything odd pop up about the Polish community?" I ask.

"Nothing yet. They're a relatively quiet bunch and, like you said, not exactly a community you connect with terrorism. There was a spree of vandalism about six months back that seemed to target Polish businesses, but nothing since."

"Were the vandals caught?"

"No record of any arrests. If they were caught, they weren't charged."

"Leave what you have on my desk and I'll take a look. Thanks."

My next call is to Mo, who runs my favorite independent cab company.

"Hey, Dix," he says before I even speak. "I hope you're not going down to the bomb site. It's a zoo. My guys are having to avoid the whole area, makes it a real bitch to get people around."

"Already been there."

"Yeah, what's the scoop?"

"Young Polish girl got caught up in something bad. You heard any rumblings?"

Mo sucks in a deep breath. "Ah, shit, a young girl? That makes me sound like a jackass for complaining. I thought it was a gas leak or something. Cops are keeping their yaps shut."

"You heard anything coming out of the Polish community lately?" I press. "Anyone new in town who might be recruiting girls?"

"No, nothing like that. All quiet as far as I know, but I can ask around."

"I'd appreciate it. I also need a cab."

"Already on its way. You know me, one foot in the grave, but keeping two steps ahead of the devil."

I laugh. "Always the poet."

"Nah, just an old cabbie." Mo chuckles, but it turns into a nasty cough as he hangs up the phone.

The taxi drops me at Mario's Deli, a hole in the wall that makes the best bagels in town. If you're not hungry, which is impossible once you smell the bagels, it also offers a discreet place where gamblers can take a flutter on anything with or without a pulse. So far, by my admittedly unreliable math skills, I'm breaking even.

Mario beams from behind the counter when I enter.

"Ms. Dixie," he calls. "Where you been hiding? We miss you so much." He glances over at his partner, Eddie the Wolf, sitting in the red vinyl booth farthest from the front door. "Eddie was saying you might be in the hospital."

"No, just keeping a low profile."

"Well, it is lovely to see you. I have something special today. Fried blood sausage on a white cheddar and cracked black pepper bagel with medium poached, free-range egg under a blanket of melted Gruyère."

"Blood sausage?" I wrinkle my nose in uncertainty.

"You ever try?"

I shake my head.

"Sit with Eddie. You don't like, it's on me. Coffee?"

I nod and move to the back booth where Eddie has barely looked up from beneath the brim of his misshapen plaid woolen cap. Behind him is a partially ajar door that leads to a back room. Directly behind the door, out of sight but never out of mind, stands Eddie's bodyguard. Having never actually seen the bodyguard, however, it could just be a story, but I've yet to pluck up the nerve to peek.

"You're alive then?" says Eddie when I sit down.

"Appears that way."

"When I heard Red Swan had withdrawn the contract, I assumed the job was done."

"We came to an understanding."

"That's unusual for Lebed."

I shrug. "I can be charming when I need to."

Eddie's eyes twitch, but I wouldn't exactly call it a smile. "It takes more than charm. Who died in your place?"

I wince. "Does it matter?"

Now it's Eddie's turn to shrug. "No."

Mario delivers my breakfast. The blood sausage is perfectly round, half an inch thick, and black as coal—like a burnt hamburger patty.

"Is it supposed to be black?" I ask.

Mario grins. "Taste. A little spicy, but in a way that will make your taste buds dance."

I look over at Eddie, but his expression hasn't changed.

I close my eyes and bite into the bagel, feeling the yolk burst and flow over the sausage. I keep my eyes closed as I chew. The texture is ... different, more granular than meaty.

"Well?" asks Mario.

"The texture is off-putting," I say. "But it tastes delicious." And it does—like a meaty, Cajun turkey dressing.

Mario beams. "See, I expand your world today."

I take another bite, this time with my eyes open, as Mario walks away.

"He's expanding my world," I tell Eddie.

Eddie's eyes twitch again and his face softens ever so slightly. "He's good at that."

In between bites, I slurp my coffee and feel my energy return. It's amazing how having a young woman explode in front of your eyes can sap your strength.

"You want to place a bet?" Eddie asks. "Greyhounds are racing this afternoon, and the Niners are at home."

"You got a list of the dogs?"

Eddie digs into a folder beside his laptop and slides over the lineup for the dog track. I spot a hound named Marmalade Spice at 20 to 1 odds, and slide Eddie ten bucks to win.

Eddie accepts the money before glancing at the sheet. "Twenty to one?" He shakes his head. "If I had a conscience, I'd feel bad about taking your money."

"Good job you don't."

"Yeah."

"One other thing."

Eddie sighs but doesn't try to stop me.

"You heard any rumblings coming out of the Polish community? Any new people moving in? Explosives, drugs, women?"

"That's a heady combo. Not my turf."

"But you have ears on the ground. The bombing this morning, you won't read about it in the papers, but the explosives were *inside* the girl. Who would do something like that?"

There's a sudden movement of feet from behind the door at Eddie's back, as though someone is growing impatient. Eddie glances over his shoulder with steely eyes. It's as if he expects someone to emerge.

"I got nothing," he says brusquely.

"You sure?"

Eddie's brow furrows. "Don't push me, Dix. I like you better than most, but even that has its limits."

I flash him a sly grin. "You like me?"

Eddie's brow furrows deeper. "What'd I just say?"

I smile wider. "You said you like me."

Eddie the Wolf practically growls.

"Time for me to go?" I ask.

Eddie remains silent as I get up, pay for my breakfast, and head into the street.

———

A surprise visit by the sun has burned away the morning fog, making passersby stand a little taller rather than hunched against the season's low ceiling. I allow the rays to heat my face for a moment, my skin sucking in its daily dose of vitamin D.

I think of Ania, the heat and pain that must have washed over her in that final second, but instead of the explosion, my mind wanders to the raw scar that ran beneath her belly.

It was a cesarean scar—and a butcher's one at that—and yet she claimed not to have children. Could skin be stretched that much to place something inside or am I missing an important part of the puzzle?

A large shadow falls over me, blocking every ray of sunshine.

"I'm told you can be trusted," says a deep voice.

I turn toward the source and find myself having to crane my neck in order to look up into a face that has a lot in common with the rectangular blade of a garden shovel.

From this angle, I can barely make out a set of dark eyes and a long, wide nose beneath the shadow of a protruding brow and eyebrows that have linked together to form a hairy barricade. Beneath the nose is a set of lips about the same size and shape as two sausage links, and a square chin.

I gulp.

"Do I know you?"

"I work for Eddie."

"Doing what?"

"This and that."

A light switches on in my brain. "You stand behind the door."

The large man shrugs. "Sometimes."

I grin and hold out my hand. "Pleased to finally meet you. I'm Dixie."

The giant swallows my hand in his and gives it a near bone-crushing squeeze. "Jakub, with a K."

"You want to go inside and chat, Jakub?" I ask, putting emphasis in the foreign pronunciation: YAH-koob.

Jakub glances inside the restaurant and shakes his head. "I'm supposed to be behind the door." He stabs his thumb in the direction of the alley that leads behind the building. "Can we talk back there? In private."

"I don't normally go into back alleys with strangers."

The giant man flashes a set of crooked teeth, each the size of my thumbnail. "It's OK," he says. "I'm no stranger, I'm Jakub."

"Ah, well then, good." How can I argue with that logic?

When Jakub turns to head down the alley, I check that Lily, my switchblade, is still tucked safely in my boot before joining him.

———

Jakub sits on the edge of a short, grease-stained wall behind the deli. A copy of *Racing Form* has been placed on the stone to protect his trousers, and at least a hundred damp cigarette butts litter the ground at his feet.

He places a fresh cigarette between his lips and lights up before folding his arms across a chest that reminds me of a rain barrel, the kind that needs to be held in check with iron bands. Although his tailored jacket is cut to fit, his biceps and shoulders strain the cloth; even sitting down, he's an imposing slab of muscle.

If he showed up at my door looking for unpaid gambling debts, I would give him every cent I had.

"You been working for Eddie a long time?" I ask just to break the ice.

Jakub shrugs. "We go back."

"You enjoy it?" I cringe inwardly at the lame question.

Jakub shrugs again. "Sometimes."

Man of few words.

"You wanted to talk?" I prod.

"Eddie says you can be trusted."

"I do my best."

"You were asking about girls. Polish girls. One is hurt?"

"She's dead," I say bluntly. "Somebody filled her belly with explosives. For what purpose, I have no idea, but I don't believe she wanted to hurt anyone."

Jakub scratches his nose with a callused knuckle while simultaneously exhaling smoke. It's like watching somebody poke a small, tentacle-less octopus, which tells me somebody at sometime fought back hard enough to destroy all the cartilage. Whether that had been enough to slow Jakub down, only his opponent would know for sure.

"Do you know her name?" he asks.

"Ania Zajak. She was a kid. Nineteen. Does that mean anything to you?"

Jakub ignores my question. "I can give you a name, but it's not for a story."

"You want it kept anonymous?"

"Yes. She's a private woman. She will talk to you if I ask, but her name must stay between us. Can I trust you?"

I stare into a pair of incredibly large eyes surrounded by the kind of generous lashes that women would kill for—so long as he didn't kill them first. "Yes."

He cracks his knuckles and I have to resist the urge to flee. The neck-snapping noise alone nearly loosens my bladder.

"Eddie doesn't like people and makes few exceptions. You are one of the exceptions. I'm not sure why."

"Probably cause I'm so darn cute," I quip.

Jakub shakes his overly large head. It's shaved and meaty, resting on a thick neck that ripples with tendons and muscle. All he needs is a ring through his nose and a pair of horns, and I'll need to whip out my red cape and yell "Ole!"

"No," says Jakub. "He responds to your fearlessness."

"I'm not that fearless."

A noise like a chuckle rumbles in Jakub's throat. "But enough so that you walk down a deserted alley with a man like me, even though you suspect what I do."

"Yeah, I'm guessing you're not the flower arranger."

Jakub shows his teeth again. I think it's a smile; at least I hope it is. "My *ciotka* runs a private clinic that caters mostly to Polish women. She tells me things that are troubling. You two should meet."

I'm intrigued. "A private clinic?"

"Very private, which must stay that way. Despite my protests, she also helps Russian immigrants when they are in trouble, and that is something that cannot be made public."

"The Red Swan?" I ask.

Jakub nods. "I would not want him knowing. He is not a friend of the Poles."

"Well, Krasnyi Lebed and I are not exactly on speaking terms."

"That is what I understand. So we have bargain?"

"One more question. What is *ciotka*?"

Jakub thinks for a moment, the term so common to him that he's likely never thought of the English translation. "Aunt," he says finally. "My father's sister. Not always a pleasant woman, but smart."

I hold out my hand and Jakub swallows it in his. I try not to grimace as he squeezes flesh to seal the deal.

FOUR

THE ADDRESS JAKUB GIVES me is nestled in the Richmond District, a multicultural neighborhood in the northwest corner of the city. Sandwiched between the Presidio and Golden Gate Park, the area is home to a sizable Chinese, Russian, and Polish population.

The taxi drops me in front of a once-elegant Victorian-style mansion with a *Room For Rent* sign in the main floor window. After the taxi leaves, I take a tentative step onto the first of six wooden stairs that lead up to the front door.

On either side of the generously wide staircase is a narrower stairwell that leads down to the windowed basement level, which in a more affluent time would have allowed the servants to accept deliveries of food, milk, and coal without disturbing the master and mistress of the house.

But the days of opulent, single-family homes are long gone in this neighborhood. Similar to the home I share, this house has been converted into suites, but I don't notice any signs that proclaim there's also a private clinic inside.

"You don't have to do this, dear," says a voice behind me.

I turn to see a neatly dressed woman in her early fifties wearing a navy blue skirt suit that appears to be about five years out of fashion. Her earlobes sparkle with fake diamond earrings that actually appear to be clip-ons, and the lipstick on her lower lip is partially nibbled away.

I check out her shoes. Polished to a shine, but years on hard pavement have taken their toll.

"What don't I have to do?" I ask.

"What you're contemplating."

"And that is?"

The woman's face reddens slightly as she reaches into her pocket and produces a pink business card. "If you call that number, we can help. There are many families who would love to have a baby to spoil and raise in comfort. How far along are you?"

I bristle and touch my stomach. There may be a slight food baby from Mario's breakfast sandwich, but ... "I'm not pregnant."

"Oh?" The woman blushes brighter. "Sorry, it's just—"

"Just what?" I snap.

"You're not local, and most women who come here on their own—"

"Are looking for abortions?" I interrupt.

"Yes."

I pluck the card out of her hand. On the front is a drawing of a smiling baby dangling in a sling from the beak of an equally happy stork. "But you offer them an alternative?" I say.

"Yes. Well … not me personally, I just hand out the cards, but the organization provides a wonderful service. They make sure all the moms-to-be are comfortable with living quarters, meals, clothes, and vitamins. Plus they offer introductions to the baby's new parents so that everybody is involved. The moms are also very well rewarded so that they can get back on their feet after the birth."

"Cash for babies?" I say.

The woman flinches. "No, no. This is saving lives. Young, innocent lives."

I slide my tongue across my teeth and pocket the card. "You hand out many of these?"

The woman offers up a smile. "I try my best to reach everyone."

"And what's your cut?"

"I-I don't—"

"Commission," I explain. "Do you get a percentage of every girl who takes you up on your offer?"

"Erm, well, no. I am paid a salary to hand out the cards. It's a service. Almost a calling, you could say."

I shake my head. "I wouldn't."

"Oh, but—"

"Thanks," I interrupt again and point at the sign in the window. "But I have an appointment to look at a room for rent."

Turning to continue up the stairs, I hear the woman scurrying back into the shadows.

Now at least I know exactly what kind of clinic I'm looking for.

———

In the lobby, I study the mailboxes to find the name Jakub gave me. Irena Krawiec lives on the top floor, which gives me time to study the house's architecture as I climb.

I wonder what the original owners did for a living, as some of the original adornments—from a time when aesthetics were as important as craftsmanship—are still visible beneath layers of cheap paint and crude renovations. The ceilings are edged in ornate cornices that appear to tell a seafaring tale with tall ships, blue whales, abundant schools of fish, and the occasional menacing giant squid, while delicate plaster roses remain in the middle of each expanse where chandeliers must have hung.

Unfortunately, half the cornices are chipped and broken and covered in whatever discount paint the renovator bought by the barrel, and the chandeliers have been replaced by glaringly bare lightbulbs.

On the second landing, an apartment door creaks open and a young boy pokes his head out to stare at me with wide-eyed curiosity. Snot is dripping from his nose in a viscous stream, but he doesn't seem to care. His eyes are the purest sapphire blue and he doesn't make a sound as I walk past him and continue up.

On the top floor, I stop to catch my breath for a second before knocking. The moment my knuckles rap on the door, a small brass cover in the shape of a flattened teardrop swivels to one side. A deep brown eye stares out at me through a crude hole drilled in the door.

I hold up a business card that identifies me as a reporter with *NOW* magazine.

"Miss Krawiec?" I ask. "My name is Dixie Flynn. Your nephew said to expect my visit."

"Jakub is good boy," says the woman.

The brass cover slides back to cover the DIY hole and the deadbolt is unlocked with an audible clunk. When the door opens, a short and hefty woman with a colorful nylon scarf tied around her head bids me entrance.

"You hungry?" she asks.

I remember the woman's comments outside and touch my stomach. "No, thanks, I ate recently."

"Coffee?"

"Always."

The woman points the way to the main room. "Go. Sit. I make us coffee."

The living room is a cluttered jumble of handiwork and solitude: knitted shawls draped over every chair, knitted dolls with woolen hair on every shelf, and a few dozen framed photographs of people looking far too serious. Most of the photos are black and white or brown sepia, but a couple of the more recent ones are in color. I spot one photo that can only be Jakub when he was a boy, looming at least a foot over four other children and looking very glum in an unflattering pair of shorts and suspenders.

"My family is not much for smiling," says Irena as she re-enters the room with a small silver tray holding two cups of black coffee. "They associate it too much with dishonesty."

"Smiling?" I ask, not sure I've heard her right.

Irena settles the tray on a small table. "The people who smile the most are salesmen, conmen, politicians, and bankers," she explains.

"My family's roots are planted firmly in the ground where the sweat on your brow reveals one's character."

"And a smile?"

"Means you're trying to hide something."

"Seems like a grim way to live."

Irena shrugs. "Poland's history has shown us the hand of friendship can easily become a fist. What do you take in your coffee?"

"A splash of cream, please."

"I have milk."

"That's fine." I automatically smile to emphasize my agreement, but then quickly cover it with my hand.

Irena glances across at me and I think I see the glimmer of a smile in her eyes, but I can't be sure.

"Where's your clinic?" I ask.

"Close by."

"You own two apartments?"

"What makes you think that?"

"A woman stopped me outside, thinking I was coming inside for a termination. And since it appears you only have one bedroom, that means your clinic must be in one of the other apartments."

"You have a busy mind," says Irena.

"That's a nice way to put it. Most people just call me nosy."

Irena hands me my coffee.

"The woman outside," I continue.

"In blue?" Irena asks.

I nod. "Do you know her?"

"She has been around for the last six months or so."

"Affecting business?"

Irena takes a sip of coffee. "Although I make money off my services, I do not consider it a business. Many of these women have no health care, no husband, and little chance of good employment. Some of them don't even have English. A baby can be an enormous burden at the wrong time in a woman's life. I have seen babies born into that situation and neither mother nor child thrive." Irena stares at me, judging, and I feel a chill in my bones. "They are not all prostitutes and addicts."

"I never said—"

"But it crosses your mind," she interrupts. "I have seen so many women who are the worst enemies to other women. They judge and scold and blame. I do not. I provide a service. I try to save lives."

"But?"

Irena stares at me in confusion.

"Jakub said something was troubling you," I explain.

"The woman in blue is a nuisance, but I cannot blame her for my recent decline in clients."

"Why not?"

"If a woman can be persuaded to go down another path, then she should pursue that course. I want every woman who walks into my clinic to have no doubt as to what will happen. The finality of it. That is also why I like being on the top floor. It gives women time to think, to make sure they do not have second thoughts."

"Does the woman in blue convince many?"

"A few perhaps, but even that . . ." She stops as though not wanting to give voice to her thoughts.

"Please," I say. "It helps if I know everything."

Irena takes another sip of coffee. I do the same and find it to be dark, thick, and vibrant on the tongue.

"We are a small community," says Irena. "Although spread throughout the city, we hear stories about which relatives are arriving, who is leaving, marriages, births, and deaths. A lot of us come from the same small villages or neighboring cities, and like most groups, we often crave the familiar, whether that is food, music, dance, or just to hear our native tongue."

"I get that," I say. "My father always keeps a bottle of Jameson Irish Whiskey around, and he's third-generation American."

Irena dismisses my interjection with a wave of her hand. "We are a community," she says sharply, "and we know when something is wrong."

"And what is wrong?" I ask, giving her my most attentive look.

"Young women are vanishing, and not just the pregnant ones. Polish women have long been exploited for their innocent beauty by evil men, but this is something more."

"You're talking about the sex trade?"

Irena shakes her head. "That's just it. The sex trade, our poor daughters and sisters smuggled into this country as slaves for the vulgar needs of men, is something that we understand. It is a thing that we try to fight as we did in our homeland against the Russians and the Nazis before them, but this is something new. The women who arrive by boat are vanishing *before* they're sold to the sex merchants, and we do not know where they go or who is taking them."

"Ania Zajak?" I ask.

Irena nods. "She is one of the disappeared."

It takes a moment to gather my thoughts before I ask, "If Ania was smuggled here illegally, what makes you say she disappeared?"

"Her aunt paid the smugglers to bring her over, but Ania never arrived. The smugglers claimed that she never made it onto the boat, but Ania could no longer be contacted in Poland. My friend did not know where she was until we read your story on the computer this morning. If Ania has been here all this time, where was she being kept and why?"

"How long ago was she supposed to have arrived?"

"Eight months."

"Can I meet the aunt?"

"It is already being arranged, but it may take several hours. Not every woman is free to roam the city as you are. More coffee?"

As I hand the woman my cup, I say, "So Jakub recommending we meet—"

Irena's eyes sparkle. "Jakub is a good boy."

FIVE

A TAXI DROPS ME as close to the barricaded crime scene as the congealed traffic allows. On my zigzag path through the thick and morbidly curious foot traffic, I stop in at the Mocha House and pick up three dark-chocolate mochas, extra hot with sprinkles but no whip.

Dixie's Tips #21: *When you need a caffeine buzz, avoid the whipped cream—it takes away precious space in the cup for more coffee. Besides, whip goes straight to the hips without satisfying a single chocolate craving.*

At the police barrier, I tell the uniform on duty that I've been instructed to bring the drinks directly to Det. Sgt. Frank Fury and the coroner, Ruth Buttersworth. The cop doesn't buy it, not even when I bat my eyelashes. Guess she must be straight—or she can tell I am.

"Can you give Fury a buzz?" I ask. "He hates when his mocha gets cold—and I'm betting he's already kinda cranky, right?"

The officer's stern face cracks at my knowledge of Frank's mood. She makes a call on her shoulder-mounted radio. When she receives a reply, she grudgingly moves the barrier to allow me access and points to a black tactical van blocking access to the multistory parking structure.

"Keep to the edge," she warns. "And don't step in any blood."

At ground level, the scene isn't quite as morbid as it appeared from six stories up, mostly because it's impossible to take in the complete horror with one glance. With the eyewitnesses processed and escorted away from the street, the scene has become less personal and more technical. Waterproof tarps cover several locations where I'm guessing larger pieces of Ania have landed, while hundreds of tiny yellow flags pinpoint blood spatters and other material deemed worthy of photographing and cataloging.

Workmen have been allowed entry to board up the broken windows of ground-level storefronts and second-floor offices, while the absence of traffic and blaring car alarms makes everything seem almost serene.

A light drizzle of rain is washing the sidewalk and road, creating rivulets of diluted pink that run in the gutters and vanish into sewers. Morbidly, I wonder if it will increase the number of shark sightings in the bay.

Before I can reach the black van, Frank steps out of the back and stretches his hands above his head to unkink his back. He sees me coming and asks, "One of those for me?"

I hand over a mocha and watch his reaction. He grimaces slightly at the first sweet sip, but it fades with the second.

"Hot chocolate with an extra caffeine kick," I say.

"It's weird, but not bad. Who's the extra one for?"

"Ruth. She still around?"

Frank tilts his head in the direction of a large white tent set up in the middle of the road. "I was just heading over."

"Any new developments?" I ask, falling into step beside him.

"Not much, except…" He pauses and stops in his tracks before turning to face me. "When did you start reporting online before you know all the facts?"

"New orders," I say, trying not to sound defensive. "Publisher wants to update our business model to compete more directly with the dailies. I didn't have a choice."

Frank grunts. "The other vultures aren't happy that you printed a name before we've released one."

"Ania told me her name. Not your fault she asked for me and not the pushy chick from Channel 4."

"This could cause some problems."

"Nothing we can't work out. I held back some pretty big details until I uncover what exactly is going on."

Frank grunts again and continues toward the tent.

"Earlier you said there was nothing new, *except?*" I press, falling into step again.

"Anything bother you about the way she exploded?" Frank asks.

"Lots of things. Why? What's bothering you?"

"Did you notice a detonator in her hand?"

I think back and shake my head. "Maybe the bomb was fitted with a mercury switch or something that was triggered when she dropped from the roof."

"Too unreliable. What if she tripped before reaching her target?" Frank shakes his head. "This device needed a detonator."

"But if Ania didn't have it—"

"Then someone else did," finishes Frank.

———

Reaching the tent, Frank orders me to remain outside while he enters. Telling a reporter not to be nosy is like placing a frosty beer in front of a thirsty drunk and expecting him not to sneak a swallow.

I sidle up close and peer through the door flap. It's difficult to make out exactly what's going on inside except that a bank of halogen lights makes it look like some kind of alien autopsy out of *The X-Files*.

Frank and Ruth are whispering to each other and I can see the coroner's smile brighten. But when she takes a step back to pull off her surgical gloves, I see something much less pleasant. Lying on the ground, bathed in a pool of bright, unflattering light, is Ania's head and upper torso. The partial torso is a torn and ragged mess that is missing everything below the rib cage. Also gone are her right breast, right arm, and left hand.

As I reel backwards in shock, my mind's eye is locked on the stump of her severed spine and the exposed dark purple meat of her motionless heart.

When Ruth steps out of the tent, she immediately rushes to my side.

"Dixie, are you okay?" she asks quickly. "You're deathly pale."

I numbly move my head.

"Frank!" Ruth barks. "Help me lower her to the ground."

Frank moves forward and places me on my rear on the wet road. "You looked in the tent, didn't you?" he says.

I hold up the extra mocha to Ruth. "I brought you a hot drink."

Ruth takes the mocha and plops down beside me. Frank refuses to sit but bends his knees into a squat.

"That's why I told you to stay outside," Frank continues, anger barely tempered by concern.

I smile weakly. "Guess I should've listened."

"How many times have I said that?"

"Shhh, Frank," chides Ruth. "Can't you see she's had a shock?"

"The only shock is that I thought she'd listen."

Ruth doesn't have to say anything more; the flash in her eyes is enough to make Frank swallow any more words he may be contemplating.

After a few moments and several sips of mocha, I feel the blood returning to my face.

Dixie's Tips #22: *Chocolate cures everything—except maybe bullet wounds. Even then, a bar of it on the way to hospital can't hurt.*

"Sorry," I say, "I wasn't expecting to see her face. The bomb ... it didn't ..."

"She was a pretty young thing wasn't she?" says Ruth, directing my thoughts away from the horror. "Just a kid really."

I nod. "Her aunt paid to have her brought over from Poland, but she went missing—until today, that is."

"Missing?" interjects Frank.

I meet his stern gaze. "Her aunt didn't know where, how, or why."

"You're looking into it?"

"Yes, but—"

"But you're going to keep me in the loop this time, right? I want the name of the aunt."

I nod sheepishly at his harsh tone. "I don't know the name yet, but I'm hoping to meet with her later today or tonight."

Frank sighs heavily. "This needs to be a two-way street, Dix. Last time you went running off on your own, people died, and I can't keep cleaning up your—"

"She gets the picture, Frank," interrupts Ruth.

Frank's eyes narrow. "I wouldn't bank on it."

I turn to Ruth. "Have you found anything?"

"Nothing official."

"Was she actually pregnant?" I press.

"At the time of the explosion?"

"Or even recently?"

Ruth moves her head in a half-shrug, half nod. "With one breast and some preliminary blood work to go on, if I had to guess, I would say there is a strong likelihood that she may have been pregnant recently. But without the rest of her body, I can't say if she ever delivered."

"So she may have a baby out there somewhere?"

Ruth reaches out to gently stroke my cheek. "I really can't say, Dix."

"But it's possible?"

Ruth sighs. "It's possible.

SIX

I RETURN TO THE office and rush up the stairs in a bid to fight off the aroma of Dmitri's cooking before it hooks me around the neck and drags me to a corner table. In a cruel test of willpower, the *NOW* office is located above a Greek restaurant where the daily lunch special is often served with a chilled glass of Domestica, grilled pita, and fresh garlicky tzatziki.

Even still suffering the aftereffects of shock, a girl's gotta eat.

I make it to my desk with only a small puddle of drool leaking from the side of my mouth, which on anyone else would be highly unattractive.

Alongside the folder of clippings from Lulu, there is a bright yellow memo from the publisher and a white box tied with a black ribbon. I glance around the room and see little evidence of other white boxes and other black ribbons.

"It's a smartphone," says Mary Jane Clooney, the paper's pretty, petite pain-in-the-ass who was recently promoted to Lifestyle editor.

She sits a couple of desks away from me. Much to her chagrin, the promotion didn't come with an office. "Publisher has ordered all staff to carry one. Most people have their own and I hear he wasn't pleased that he had to pay for yours."

"I prefer pay phones," I say.

Mary Jane wrinkles her nose. "You're such a dinosaur."

"I prefer the term *classic*."

"There is nothing classic about a public urinal being used by drug dealers and vagrants."

"Drug dealers are too paranoid to trust pay phones these days. They use burners now."

"And you would know."

I show her my teeth. "Don't diss ma peeps, beyotch."

Mary Jane rolls her eyes. "I don't even know what that means, but it sounds racist."

I roll my eyes back at her. "You're far too white to pull out the race card, MJ. Besides, the best thing about pay phones is that when I need to call you, I can always find your number scrawled on the wall. Much easier than sneaking into a men's room."

With a shocked inhale of breath and a squeak that reaches a pitch higher than human hearing, Mary Jane spins back to her computer. I push the box aside and open the folder of clippings instead. Lulu has done her usual excellent job, but there's nothing in the articles that even hints at missing girls or illegal smuggling in the Polish community.

I'm about to return the files to the morgue when a large shadow descends over my desk. I look up into the folds of Stoogan's chins.

"Hey boss, you lose some weight or you just unhappy to see me?"

Only two of his chins smile, but the ripples fade before reaching his lips. "Have you read the publisher's memo?"

"Mary Jane gave me the crib notes. She's big into cribs, it's a cougar thing."

Mary Jane rewards my cheekiness with an annoyed clacking of her tongue.

Dixie's Tips #23: *Never assume you're ever out of earshot of a journalist—even a dull one like Mary Jane. Like bats, our ears can swivel in all directions regardless of where we're actually looking.*

"New mandate," says Stoogan. "All reporters must carry a smartphone."

"Will it actually make us smarter though?" I ask. "Because I have a theory. How many people know their friends' phone numbers anymore? If Mary Jane lost her phone, I bet she wouldn't know what number to call in an emergency."

"911," Mary Jane calls out in disgust.

"I was thinking more of a real emergency, like if you discovered a wrinkle on your forehead or one of your boobs deflated."

"Enough!" squeaks Stoogan as Mary Jane makes a loud, unladylike noise with her throat and stomps away from her desk with the *click-clack* of stiletto heels, which even I have to admit is a great way to stomp away. My boots don't so much *click* as *thud*, and if it's been raining hard, they *squelch*. Nobody takes you seriously if you *squelch* away.

"Must have been something you said," I tell Stoogan.

He growls and sighs simultaneously. "Training will be offered over the next few days. I want you to attend a session and learn what it can do, especially the camera and voice recording. It should be on your person at all times so that we can reach you."

"You miss me that much?" I quip. "That's touching, boss, really. But doesn't a leash usually come with a nice collar? You know, something in leather with chrome studs that spell out Rover or Butch or something."

Stoogan's ghostly eyebrows twitch like emaciated caterpillars on cocaine, but he chooses not to rise to the bait. "It's been set up with your e-mail and my direct line. Learn to use it."

"Way ahead of you." I hold up my trigger finger. "This little finger does the dialing." I fold the finger back into my palm and hold up my thumb. "And this digit says great job."

Stoogan exhales through his nose as though trying to dislodge a stubborn booger. "It'll also help if you take it out of the box."

"You should be in IT." I grin. "You definitely have the physique for it."

With a final, frustrated sigh, Stoogan heads back to his office. He'll thank me later; I'm the only one left in this homogenized newsroom who keeps him on his toes with the reminder that journalists aren't meant to fit in. We don't enter this profession because we want to please authority figures; we choose it because we want to challenge them, to unearth their dirty little secrets and hold them accountable for any dishonest or reprehensible action.

What's the point in having a watchdog if it rolls over and exposes its belly every time someone commands it?

Of course it's become more difficult to remain independent as publishers no longer rise from the journalism ranks. Instead, they are birthed, fully formed and without the restraints of conscience, from managerial pods in sales. To them, readers (and the stories that attract them) are unnecessary—so long as the advertisers don't realize that nobody is reading their publications anymore.

I slip off the ribbon and open the box. The phone is about the size of a chocolate bar except glossy white, inedible, and with a fully-charged battery at its core. I drop the included charger into my coat pocket, slip the phone into my front pocket, and head to the morgue to drop off Lulu's folder before giving in to temptation and heading downstairs.

———

Over lunch—where Dmitri serves up a spicy calamari and green-tomato relish po'boy sandwich with Greek salad and extra olives on the side—I pull the phone out of my pocket. Instantly, a message appears on the screen from Stoogan. It reads: *Test*.

I tap the reply button and type: *Like a virgin, text'd for the very first time.* I don't know how to enter musical notes to indicate that Stoogan should sing my reply, preferably aloud while wearing his boxers outside of his pants in front of the publisher—so I simply hit send.

Since I have the phone in hand, I enter Frank's direct line, Mo's Cabs, and Pinch into my contacts. Over a second glass of wine (since the first went down so well) I enter the numbers for both my parents, because only having four contacts seems pathetic. Good job I'm not on Twitter or Facebook, otherwise I might start to question if I actually exist.

It has become a philosophical dilemma in this social media age: if you post something profound and nobody clicks Like, have you actually been heard?

As the wine diminishes more rapidly than I would like, I dig out the scrap of paper that Irena Krawiec handed me with her number scrawled on it. I use the new phone to dial and the perils of technology suddenly become crystal clear: How does anyone ever make it into the office when you can conduct business without leaving the bar?

Irena answers with a clipped tone. "*Cześć*? Hello? I do not know this number."

"I don't know it either," I say. "New phone and I forgot to ask what the number is."

"*Pani* Flynn?"

"Yes, I got to keep my name. Good job too; I've had this one so long I'd be screwed trying to learn a new one now."

"Have you been drinking?"

I laugh. "Yes, but I can't use that as an excuse. My sense of humor is just as odd when I'm sober." I clear my throat and take a large swallow of water. "Sorry," I say in a more professional tone, "it's been a difficult day. I went back to the scene of the bombing. The police will want Ania's aunt to identify her remains."

"Identify?"

"Part of her escaped the blast." I picture Ania's partial torso lying on the ground beneath the white tent: her bloodless face, milky dead eyes, her mouth slack and devoid of expression except what my own imagination wants to plant upon it. In my mind's eye, I draw a white sheet to just below her chin. "With the right mortician, you could hold an open casket. I know a few good people locally if you need someone."

"*Dziękuję*. I will pass along."

"Has the aunt agreed to meet with me?"

"She has, but—" Irena goes silent.

"But?" I press.

"I have been asking around."

"And?"

"The Russian ordered price on your head, but then it was no more. Is true?"

I take a sip of wine, wondering where this is going. "Yes."

"If I can ask, why did he open contract?"

"I was helping two sisters find their missing father. The trail led to the Red Swan's door, but he didn't like my snooping."

"And, more importantly, why was it cancelled?"

I hesitate and take another sip, allowing the wine's acidic bite to glide over my tongue and massage my words.

Finally, "A friend struck a bargain."

"Of blood?"

"Yes."

"And it has been paid?"

"Yes."

"*Dobrze*, good."

"Why is that good?"

"It say you not afraid to get dirty hands."

"Not if I believe in the cause."

"*Doskonały*. We meet tonight and would like for you to join us."

"Us?"

"A concerned group."

"Will Ania's aunt be there?"

"*Tak* ... Yes."

"Then count me in."

Irena gives me an address and a time before hanging up.

SEVEN

AFTER FILING AN ONLINE update on the bombing story to keep the competition riled, I drop in on one of the information sessions about how to properly use a smartphone in the new frontier of cyborg journalism.

The too-young, too-hipster-sock-wearing instructor annoys me immediately by enthusiastically telling us that the camera built into each device turns every reporter into a photojournalist.

Unfortunately, my guffaw interrupts his train of thought.

"You disagree?" he asks in the type of superior voice that gets under my skin.

"Yeah," I sneer. "Your father could have said the same thing to photojournalists about the portable typewriter or first laptop. Having the tool doesn't make you a writer, no more than having a chisel makes you Michelangelo. Great photojournalists may use cameras to capture what they see, but it's imagination, skill, and nerve that deliver front-page shots."

The instructor bristles. "I'm not arguing that, but a lot of journalism is being in the right place at the right time and with—"

"Being in the right place isn't about luck," I interrupt. "A good journalist plans ahead to put herself in that place at that time. Skill is holding your shit together long enough to get the shot while everyone around you is panicking, or finding that angle nobody else has thought of. With these phones we may get a few lucky shots on occasion, but that doesn't make us photojournalists."

"Are you a photographer?" the instructor asks, his eyes swiveling around the room for support, but finding none.

I smile thinly. "Nope."

"Then why are—"

"Because I hate when people spout off in the belief that professions can be replaced with technology. Great photography, like great writing, is a skill that demands respect. Don't belittle it."

The room falls silent as Stoogan appears on the other side of the glass wall that separates the boardroom, where the class is being taught, from the newsroom. He doesn't say a word, but his looming presence makes the other reporters nervous.

I step down from my pulpit. "OK. What else can this miracle of modern tech do?"

———

In the lobby of my apartment building, I stop to check the mail. A third package wrapped in the same red paper as the others is waiting for me. This one is a similar shape to the second parcel: long and skinny.

Lost in troubled thought, I jump when someone unexpectedly clears his throat beside me.

"Sorry, Miss Flynn," blurts the diminutive Mr. French, whose apartment door is adjacent to the mailboxes. "I didn't mean to startle you."

"It's been one of those days," I say as I begin breathing again. "Has me on edge."

"The bombing?" he asks. "I've been listening to the news. Very disturbing. They're saying a young woman was involved, which is rare for attacks on US soil."

"Don't believe everything you hear."

"Oh? It wasn't a woman?"

"No, they got that part right, but I'm not convinced it was exactly an attack. At least not of the terrorist variety."

"Ah." Mr. French smiles mischievously and plays with the edge of his new platinum mustache, which he has been grooming with special Parisian wax to make its ends curl. "When you're ready to divulge, Baccarat and I are all ears."

I laugh. "Will do. By the way, have you noticed anyone other than our regular guy dropping off mail?"

Mr. French's eyebrows arch in curiosity. "No. Why?"

"Long shot." I show him the red package. "This looks like it's been mailed, but—"

"It was sent anonymously?" he jumps in, excitement clear on his face.

I nod.

"Do you know what it is?" he asks.

"Another piece of a puzzle."

"Ah." He rubs his small hands together in glee. "You have the most interesting mysteries, Miss Flynn. If you need my help, you know you only have to ask."

"Even after last time?"

His smile fades slightly as his expression turns deadly serious. "*Especially* after last time. I know I was a little shook up when I first saw the news, and I hope this doesn't sound too self-serving, but your friendship and your trust make me feel ten feet tall."

"As does yours," I say, and mean it.

"Besides," he adds. "Danger is my new middle name."

We both laugh as Mr. French holds out a hand. "Why don't you give me that wrapping paper and I'll see what answers I can glean."

I unwrap the package and hand him the paper. The sealed white box inside contains no hint as to its contents, but I've already guessed what it's likely to contain.

———

Prince wraps himself around my ankles the moment I enter the apartment. His purr is so loud that I wonder if I forgot to feed him this morning.

One glance at his bowl in the kitchen tells me that in my rush to get out the door after Frank's emergency phone call, I either did forget to make the poor kitten breakfast or he's entering a growth spurt. Considering the size of his father—my landlady Mrs. Pennell's orange tabby, King William—and his massive paws, I have a feeling he's going to be a lovable monster.

"You hungry, my prince?" I ask as I scoop him up in my arms.

Prince's purr increases in volume as he headbutts my forehead and scrapes his sandpaper tongue along the length of my nose. The look in his eyes as he stares deep into mine is one of pure adoration.

If only I could find a man who loved me that soundly.

I fill Prince's bowl and freshen his water, adding an ice cube, since it makes him happy to bat it around with his paw and lick it while it melts.

With Prince settled, I open the white box. Inside is a short red bar that fits at a ninety-degree angle into a slot near the top of the vertical pole I received in the second package to form a gallows. There is also a third letter that I add to the existing row. The hangman's word now spells DIX_ _ with two letters to go.

I may not be Vanna White, but I'm pretty sure I can solve it already. My main concern is what happens after the puzzle is complete.

———

I lay on the couch and contemplate having forty winks to make up for my early morning and to rest for the evening ahead when the apartment phone rings.

Ignoring it is my first reaction, but since the wireless handset is lying on the Ms. Pac-Man coffee table within reach, I decide to check the caller ID. With a groan, I arm-wrestle my conscience before clicking the button and saying, "Hey, Mom."

"How many times have I told you the big city is dangerous?" my mother says without preamble.

"Every time you call."

"And that's because I worry like all good mothers should. I heard about the bombing. Are you OK?"

"I'm fine, Mom. Really."

"The newsman with the toupee said it was downtown, and I know you work downtown. Were you in the area?"

"Yes, but—"

"I knew it. I felt it in my bones. I called your father and he said not to bother you, that you would call if you needed us, but then he's a man and they're useless, really. We should keep them all on a farm and just milk the young ones as needed. Waste of space, the rest of them."

"Thanks," I say dryly. "Every daughter loves to hear their mother talk about milking young men."

"You mark my words. Once we get a woman in the White House, we'll need trim the herd, starting with these silver foxes. Can you believe they call themselves that? Silly old fools with their Viagra and hair gel. Marcy saw your father looking at convertibles on the BMW lot last week. BMW, Dixie! He should be looking at electric scooters not sports cars."

"Dad's not ready for a scooter yet, Mom. He's still perfectly mobile."

"And why is that? Because I made sure he ate properly and got regular exercise and didn't spend all his spare time hanging out with those so-called friends of his on the golf course. Drinking buddies, more like. And what thanks do I get? Divorce papers."

I wince. "I know it hurts, but I don't want to take sides. You've been separated for nearly a year now; divorce is the next step. When did Dad file?"

"Oh, he didn't. No, that would be far too much trouble. He left it up to me as usual."

"So you filed for divorce?"

"Yes. See how he likes it."

"Is that really what you want, though? If Dad didn't file, maybe—"

"Oh, don't start. You're always taking his side."

"I'm not taking sides, Mom! It's just—"

"Marcy says a clean break is best. Rip off the Band-Aid and get on with healing."

"That can be true, Mom. But you have to ask yourself, how happy is Marcy?"

A long pause is followed by a voice that holds a tremor of hurt. "I have to go, dear. I'll tell your father that you're alright."

"Mom, I didn't mean—"

The phone goes dead.

Shit! Nothing like a dose of guilt to make an afternoon nap seem like a bad idea.

I phone Frank instead. When he answers, I say, "Feel like shooting something?"

"Can't. We're going through video footage from the time of the bombing. But I'm sure Benny will be happy to see you. He told me the other day he has something he's excited to show you."

"Oh yeah? Any hints?"

"Only that, in his words, it's cool."

"I like the sound of that. Anything interesting showing up on the videos so far?"

"Not that I can discuss. Later."

My next call is to Pinch. "Feel like shooting something?"

"Always."

EIGHT

I meet Pinch outside Duck!, a private members' gun range housed in a discreet corrugated steel Quonset hut in an industrial park near the docks. Although it caters almost exclusively to law enforcement and private security, exceptions are made if you have the right references. Naturally, Frank is my reference.

Pinch hesitates at the front door, which at only five-feet-six-inches tall is what gives the club its unusual name.

"Cops and I don't usually mingle," says Pinch.

"We're not mingling, we're shooting. Besides, you're retired again, right?"

"I still prefer avoiding people who may want to shoot me one day."

"Where do you usually practice?"

"Abandoned quarries are best, but anywhere remote."

"And do they serve cold beer there?"

"Not unless you bring your own."

"Well, just pretend you're my caddy."

Pinch flashes me a stern look.

I can't help but laugh. "It'll be fine. The people most likely to want to shoot you are practicing in quarries. This is the last place they'd expect you to be."

"There's a certain logic to that."

"Of course there is." I hold open the door. "After you."

Pinch doesn't have to duck as he enters, but I have to tilt my head slightly—mostly to avoid getting my don't-give-a-damn hair caught in any cracks in the top frame.

Inside, the Quonset looks more like a gentleman's smoking club—oak, chrome, and glass with comfortable chairs, plasma TVs, and a small coffee and juice bar—with the unusual addition of soundproofing foam and bulletproof acrylic windows that look onto twelve shooting lanes.

"Hey, Dix!" Benny calls from behind the gun bar. "You bring the Governor?"

"No, this is my friend, Pinch. He's an ambassador."

Benny guffaws before I hold up my gun case and watch the excited gleam in his eye dial up a few watts.

"Never leave home without it," I add.

"Bring it over," he gestures. "I got something you're going to love."

As we approach the bar, I introduce the two men.

Benny eyes Pinch up and down, taking in every square inch of his solid, fireplug frame—not fooled in the slightest by his tailored suit jacket over a pair of expensive black jeans, soft bamboo T-shirt, and sharp-toed Fluevog shoes.

"What you shootin'?" he asks suspiciously.

Pinch shrugs. "Depends on my mood, but for close-up work, I keep going back to the Beretta 92FS in nine mil, or the 87 in twenty-two." He fixes his gaze on Benny's and holds it, reading him back. "But it's not the gun, is it?"

A smile creeps across Benny's face. "That's why I stick with the Colt. If the fucker jams, it still makes a damn good hammer." He holds out a callused hand. "Welcome to Duck! Any friend of Dixie's is welcome in my house."

Pinch accepts his hand and squeezes.

"Well this is lovely, boys," I interrupt. "But never tell a lady you have something cool to show her and then get into a dick-measuring contest. It's a real turn-off."

Benny guffaws and releases Pinch's hand. "Give me the Governor, Dix."

"Why?"

"I'm going to make it even sweeter."

I place the gun case on the counter and Benny pulls a small black box from under the counter along with a short screwdriver. Before I can protest, he's removing the factory grips from the gun and replacing them with a new pair.

When he's done, he holds the gun up in profile. "See anything new?"

"There's a button on the front and a small nub behind the barrel."

Benny grins wider as he points the empty gun toward his stock room and squeezes the new button on the front. An intense crimson dot appears exactly where he's pointing.

"It's accurate up to fifty feet," he says excitedly. "Try it on the range and tell me what you think."

"I have a feeling I'm going to love it."

Benny beams. "It's cool, ain't it?" He turns to Pinch. "Anything you want to try?"

"I brought my own."

Benny's forehead crinkles into a frown. "You don't look to be carrying."

"That's the point."

"Come on," I interrupt. "Let's try this bad girl out."

Benny's forehead remains crinkled as Pinch and I head through the door to the range.

———

The tiny laser sight proves to be just as accurate as Benny promised. By squeezing the button with my middle finger, the crimson laser allows me to land every bullet exactly where I want.

The poor silhouette doesn't stand a chance as I cluster four in the heart and one right between its eyes. When I switch to shells—the beauty of the Governor is that it can accept both .45 cartridges and .410 shotgun shells simultaneously—the laser doesn't make as much of a difference as the impact pattern is so devastatingly large.

Pinch, on the other hand, seems to be off his game until I realize he's hitting the target exactly where he wants to. Instead of aiming for center mass, he's clustering his shots in odd places: the neck, stomach or off to one side, missing the meat of the target completely.

If you didn't know him, you would assume he was a lousy shot.

When we're finished and retrieved all our paper targets, Pinch folds his carefully and slips them into his pocket rather than dropping them into the recycling bin by the door. He does the same with his spent brass.

I flash him a curious look, but he's giving nothing away.

As soon as we reappear in the clubhouse, Benny leans over the counter. "Well?"

"How much?" I ask.

"Two seventy-five, but I'll supply free batteries."

I nibble my lower lip, wondering if I can afford to splurge. "Installments?"

Benny laughs. "Twenty bucks a week until paid. Can't ask for fairer and that's only because I like you."

I hold out my hand. "Deal."

Benny shakes on it, then asks, "Two beers?"

Pinch nods and pays for the drinks before leading the way to a quiet table in the far corner beneath the stuffed head of a tusked boar wearing a leather eyepatch.

"So," I begin once we're settled, "what was with the awkward shooting?"

"For you, this is a game. Not so for me. The only people who need to know how good I am are already in their graves. I don't like to leave footprints."

"Paranoid much?"

He doesn't smile. "I'm still alive."

I take a long sip of beer before asking, "You haven't been sending me little gifts, have you?"

He puts his beer down on the table and leans forward. "What kind of gifts?"

"There have been three so far." I describe them.

"It's not me."

"What about the Red Swan?"

"He doesn't send warnings and he wouldn't break our deal."

"Why not? He's not exactly the—"

"I would kill him," interrupts Pinch. "He knows that."

As more day shifts end, more people arrive to fill up the shooting lanes. I can sense Pinch becoming edgy, although his exterior remains perfectly calm.

"You want to leave and grab a bite somewhere?" I ask.

He doesn't bother to finish his beer before heading for the door.

———

We pick up some spicy pork tacos from a food truck and find an empty bench in a local park. After making sure there are no used syringes stuck between the slats, we settle back and dig in to our Korean fusion take-out.

As the aroma drifts, addicts and panhandlers rise from the bushes nearby, but while their noses twitch, something keeps them from approaching, a sixth sense earned through experience and pain that tells them Pinch prefers to be left unmolested.

"This is the easiest way to be invisible on a busy street," says Pinch as he chews. "By remaining still, you become a blur to the world rushing by."

"Really? I would think the opposite."

"Most people would, but everyone is in such a hurry that any object that doesn't move and isn't blocking our path can be ignored. For efficiency, our brains block it out."

"Like a cat," I say. "They stay perfectly still until the moment of attack."

"Or a purse snatcher." Pinch points across the street to where a young man is window shopping with his back to the crowd. "He's watching in the reflection of the glass, waiting for the right victim." He moves his head a fraction of an inch. "His partner is over there."

"What makes you think—"

Before I can finish the question, the man spins from his position by the window, bumps a woman with his elbow and snatches the mobile phone she is holding to her ear. Before she has time to scream for help, he passes the phone onto his partner—like a baton-runner in a relay—who tears down an alleyway and is gone.

"How did you know that was going to happen?" I ask.

"The bigger question is why are you surprised? What does your mother always tell you when she calls?"

"The city is dangerous."

"She's not wrong."

I think it over for a moment before asking, "Do you keep track of the criminal element here?"

"In what way?"

"The bombing this morning. The explosives were inside a young Polish woman. Who would do that?"

"Inside?"

"She looked pregnant, but it wasn't a baby."

Pinch stops eating and looks over at me with concern. "You saw this woman?"

I nod.

"You talked to her?"

71

I nod again.

"How were you there?"

"She asked to see me before she jumped from the top of a six-story parking ramp."

"But she didn't give you the name of who did that to her?"

"No. That's why—"

"People who use explosives don't follow rules," interrupts Pinch in a voice that sends a chill down my spine. "They don't care who they hurt or how many. Collateral damage is just a nice way of saying 'we don't give a fuck.' Be careful on this one, Dix. Bombers are the lowest of the low. In my trade, we have a joke: How do you tell an amateur bomber from the professional? The professional is only missing one hand."

NINE

THE TAXI DROPS ME on a dark street outside a small bakery with crumb-free wicker trays filling its front window. The shop is closed, but a handwritten sign on the door informs me that fresh bread is available every day beginning at 5:30 a.m.

Even though it hasn't been that long since I was eating Korean tacos in the park with Pinch, the thought of crusty sourdough warm from the oven makes my salivary glands fill my mouth with drool. Even in San Francisco, finding a good sourdough is a challenge.

"Follow," says Irena Krawiec as she appears out of nowhere to brush past me on the sidewalk.

I fall in step behind her, thinking it would have been funny if she had said "swallow" instead.

She's dressed very differently—army surplus pants and jacket, hair tucked under a green knitted cap, and sturdy hiking boots—and walking with a determined kick to her step as though a younger woman has slipped under her skin. Back in her apartment, she struck me as a farm-wife tough and barn-educated woman who ran an off-the-grid abortion clinic because she didn't have a license to go legit.

But the woman walking in front of me now is standing taller and moving with a purpose that tells me I may have gravely underestimated both her age and grit.

"Where are we going?" I ask.

"Not far."

"Are you a real doctor?"

"What is real?"

"Educated. MD."

"*Tak*, of course."

"Then why run a street clinic instead of working in a hospital?"

"The women who come to me cannot visit a hospital."

"It can't be easy staying off the grid."

Irena glances over her shoulder. "Are you armed?"

Taken aback, I blurt, "Only with my wits."

"Stay close."

Irena ducks into an alley with me close on her heels. Halfway down, we turn into a narrower side alley that leads to a rusted steel door. Irena knocks twice and waits.

When the door creaks open, the space beyond is empty and dark without even a dim lightbulb to guide the way.

Dixie's Tips #24: *When a near-stranger invites you down a dark alley and into an even darker room, it's time to turn and run—unless you're a stubborn reporter with a streak of curiosity that too often blinds common sense.*

I follow Irena into the dark hallway and try not to jump when the door slams behind me and a female voice says, "*Przepraszam*, damn thing is heavy as tank."

A light finally appears farther down the hall as an interior door is opened. Irena leads me to it with the other woman following close behind. When I glance over my shoulder, the woman flashes me half a grin. The other half of her face is hidden in deep shadow, but there's something off about it, almost as if—

"Inside, *śpiesznie*." Irena gestures anxiously at the doorway to the lit room.

I enter to find the room mostly bare except for four women who turn to stare. Each woman is wearing army surplus clothes and matching green watch caps. Two of them are standing at a small table, cleaning and loading a ragtag cache of handguns and shotguns that look like they were scavenged from a Salvation Army bin.

"I take it this isn't your knitting club," I say to Irena as she moves up beside me.

The woman who followed us inside snickers. When I turn to show my appreciation, I see what was bothering me about her grin. The lower left side of her face is a distorted mess of melted flesh: cracks of bright pink peek from beneath rigid and crusty scabs of charcoal.

"I'm Dixie," I say.

The woman appears to be no older than twenty-five and has an effervescence about her that makes my heart weep for what has been done to her face—and recently.

She touches her chest with one hand. "Berta."

Irena introduces me to the other women: Julita, Krystyna, Zofia, and Matylda.

"Matylda is Ania's *ciotka*, her aunt," says Irena.

"I'm sorry for your loss," I say, crossing the floor to offer my hand.

"You were with Ania at the end?" Matylda asks.

"Yes, she asked for me to be there. I was hoping to talk her out of jumping. This was before anyone knew what had been placed inside her."

Matylda's eyes grow dark. "Irena say you saw her after also."

I wince and nod.

"How is she?" Matylda asks.

"At peace." It may not be exactly true, but there are times when a bad lie is easier than a blunt truth.

Matylda spits on the floor. "My *siostrzenica* will never be at peace until we find the *skurwysyn* who did this to her." She turns to the women tending the guns. "Pack up." And to the woman who was introduced as Zofia: "Get the van."

"Where are we going?" I ask.

"There is a delivery tonight," says Irena. "We hope you would join us."

"A delivery?" I ask.

"Of women," adds Berta.

"Not all women," says Matylda with a sneer. "The pigs cannot even wait until they bleed."

I glance over at the two women who are placing the loaded weapons into two zippered duffel bags. "And we're going armed?"

"These *dziwotwór*," says Matylda, "do not listen to words." She points over at Berta. "Tell her what you do to deserve such punishment."

Berta looks down at the floor. "I-I get nervous when I-I..." She covers her mouth to control a giggle. "An' I laughed at somebody's..." She giggles again, but it's hot with pain, not humor.

"They do delivery," interrupts Matylda with venom in her voice, "these *dziwotwór* who call themselves men. They take Berta and other girls around construction sites for sex. Berta laughed at one of the men when he dropped his pants. Thinking she was insulting his *męskość*, he grabbed the closest thing, a bucket of bubbling roof tar."

"I was lucky," adds Berta.

"Lucky?" I ask.

"Berta was able to break free of her handler before the tar covered her completely," adds Matylda. "Her handler took most, and in his pain, he shot the worker."

"He begged me to go for help," says Berta.

"Fortunately, she found us instead," finishes Matylda.

"You will come with us?" Berta asks. "We're concerned they may have extra men because of this morning."

Wishing I had brought the Governor, I say, "Try and stop me."

———

In the back of the van, we try not to stare at each other as every bump in the road reverberates through the bare metal floor and into our cramped muscles and bones. The women had offered me a spare set of baggy army fatigues to slip over my clothes and a matching watch cap.

I think of Frank and try to imagine how pissed he will be if he ever finds out what I've agreed to be part of. Then again, the only way he'll find out is if everything goes pear-shaped, which I'm trying to convince myself is not as likely as the ragtag crew and Salvation Army weapons indicate.

"How are the women shipped in?" I ask to break the silence.

"By boat," says Irena. "Large shipping containers with hidden rooms in back."

"If lucky," pipes in Berta.

"What do you mean?" I ask her.

"My container did not have a room. It was lined with false walls so that box was narrower inside than it looked from outside. Each of us had to stand in slots between the walls in space smaller than coffin. It was like being buried alive."

"How long did you have to stay like that?" I ask.

"I lose track. We ran out of water, but nobody could move. The space was so tight, some of the fatter ones couldn't breathe. Their death mix with the stench of our stewing bodies."

"Women died?"

Berta shrugs. "It happens. They tell you it won't. That you will be treated nice, but all men are liars."

"*Skurwiele koza*," spits Matylda.

"Goat fuckers," translates Irena, just in case I missed the sentiment.

"How many women?" I ask Berta.

"We begin our travel with group of perhaps thirty, and maybe twenty of us make it out of the container."

"Jesus," I gasp.

"For some," Berta continues, "the dead are lucky. These are not nice men."

I turn to Irena. "You know the location of this new shipment?"

Irena nods. "The ship arrived two nights ago. I am told tonight is pickup."

"Who tells you?" I ask.

"Some men are not as evil as others, but very few. Those who cannot look away find a need to unburden. We have ears to listen."

"*Skurwiele koza*," repeats Matylda, which makes me think she doesn't share Irena's opinion on men.

Irena shrugs. "Perhaps," she answers her friend, "but we are here now because of one."

The van slows as we enter a turn and the rhythm of paved tarmac becomes the crunch of gravel. Julita and Krystyna open the duffel bags on the floor.

"You have a preference?" asks Julita in perfect, unaccented American.

"Shotgun." Although I'm becoming a decent shot with the Governor, a shotgun is a more intimidating weapon when you're feeling as nervous as I am.

Julita passes over a manhandled, double-barreled Remington that's been crudely cut down for close-contact mayhem by someone with no appreciation of weapons.

"Ammunition is tight," she says, passing over a handful of shells. "So make them count."

Before I can begin to question myself, the van stops and the rear doors slide open.

TEN

THE NIGHT BREEZE IS cold on my flesh, raising goosebumps despite the sweat trickling beneath my clothes. A thin blanket of fog swirls around us, breaking into semisolid wisps that skip and laugh like demonic children playing a ghostly game of Catch Me If You Can.

Matylda leads us along the perimeter of an imposing twelve-foot fence topped with unnerving curls of razor wire. Beyond the fence lies a maze containing hundreds of multicolored shipping containers stacked three to four high. As a unit, we slink into deeper darkness behind a disheveled row of dilapidated containers that have been cast out of the main yard like sickly metallic whales and left to rust. Despite generations of taggers leaving their mark in fluorescent paint, the salt-eaten metal crumbles into flecks of orange and brown at a single touch.

Behind the containers, Matylda kneels down and instantly begins to unravel a mended breech in the wire fence that she's obviously used before.

It's only a few minutes until the near-invisible stitch is undone and a flap large enough to crawl through is folded back. One by one, our ragtag team of women drop to our stomachs and wiggle through. Matylda enters last, while Zofia expertly folds the flap back in place before returning to keep watch over the van in case we need to make a quick getaway.

"Keep to dark paths," warns Matylda. "The company guards should be paid to stay away, but if these *dziwotwór* are expecting trouble, they maybe brought more."

We all nod as though the prospect of running into armed guards sounds perfectly reasonable, and then we're off, darting from container to container, heading deeper into the yard towards—

Matylda freezes and holds up her hand to stop us in our tracks. She points toward a stand of portable, battery-powered lights glowing a short distance away, and over the loud beating of my heart I hear male voices arguing.

Matylda makes a circling motion with her finger and the women spread out in practiced formation with the goal of arriving at the lit spot from different directions. I freeze in place, not sure what I'm meant to do before Berta taps me on the shoulder and indicates that I should join her.

Berta leads me in a wide half-circle so that we end up approaching the lit spot from behind. When we're only one container away,

Berta holds up her hand for us to stop and wait. Crouching down, I touch her shoulder to let her know that I have her back.

A short distance in front of us, two men are arguing in a broken mixture of Polish and English, but their relaxed body language tells me it's about something insignificant.

"Football," Berta whispers. "Every man has opinion about being better coach."

"Are the women here?" I whisper back. "Can you see them?"

"*Nie*, but these two are guarding something."

Adrenaline surges through my body, making every limb twitchy and anxious to move. A feral impulse causes my lips to curl back and expose my teeth. My heart races and I worry that if we don't move soon, I may end up howling at the invisible moon.

Suddenly, the two men spring to attention as a disembodied male voice yells "*Przenieść,* go," followed by the unsettling sound of whimpering.

Peering intently over Berta's shoulder, I watch more than a dozen frightened women shuffle out of a bruised scarlet container and into the open square of light. They look even worse than I imagined they would and I wonder how many days they have spent locked up in that metal box without sanitation, food, or enough water to drink.

Feeling the heat of my outrage, Berta reaches back to touch my hand that is unconsciously digging into her shoulder. I apologize and release my taloned grip.

"Be ready to move."

She doesn't have to tell me twice.

When the third man appears with the last of the women—I count eighteen in total—he's not alone. A fourth walks beside him and, surprisingly, he's someone I've met before. A gristly longshoreman with bad teeth and overgrown mutton-chop sideburns, his name, if I remember correctly, is Gerek. I accidentally broke his finger and purposefully broke his nose when he tried to pinch my ass in a bar in one of the sleaziest hotels in the city.

I was looking for a prostitute at the time in the hotel owned by the Red Swan, and it seems my low opinion of its patrons was more than warranted.

All four men are armed with modern, pump-action Mossberg shotguns that look fresh from the box. Gerek has his slung over his shoulder to leave his hands free to wield an electric cattle prod. As I watch, he touches the prod to the doors of the metal container and snickers mirthlessly as blue sparks fly into the air with a menacing crackle. In reaction, the frightened women scurry together into a tight terrified bunch, which tells me they've seen up close what this device can do to the human nervous system.

Berta creeps forward, slowly and stealthily, hugging the darkness, with me glued to her heels and anxious to be let loose.

The leader of the men spits on the ground as he walks around the pack of terrified women, his fingers reaching out to pinch a cheek or squeeze an arm, leg, or breast.

"Bah!" he grunts aloud to no one in particular. "These *dziwka* are even worse than last month. Are there no sexy women left in Poland?"

His three companions laugh in unison, but their mirth is cut short when Matylda enters the circle of light with a shotgun tight against her shoulder and aimed square at the chest of the leader.

"*Skurwiele koza*," she snarls.

The leader barely flinches, although his cohorts freeze in shocked confusion when Irena joins her friend in the light. Irena is armed with twin revolvers—a .45 and a smaller .38—each pointing at a different man.

"Now," says Berta as she rushes forward.

The two guards closest to us turn slightly at the sound of our approach, but their attention is distracted by two other armed women—Julita and Krystyna—rushing in from the side.

Without a moment's hesitation, I smash the butt end of my sawn-off shotgun into the side of one guard's neck and sweep his leg away with a sharp blow to the back of his knee. I expect to hear a scream as his knee audibly pops, but the blow to his neck has taken away his voice and he collapses without so much as a whimper.

As he twitches on the ground, I twist the shiny new shotgun out of his hands to replace my more limited weapon.

When I return my attention to the scene around me, everyone is staring. Nobody else, it seems, has thought to lay a beating on the guards.

"Take their guns," I order with more force than I intend, but I'm angry that these women believe the element of surprise and superior numbers guarantee success. When it comes to a gun battle, never leave your enemy time to plan, and never, ever leave their weapons within reach. Pinch taught me that.

Passing my discarded sawn-off to Berta, I stomp over to where Gerek is standing with the cattle prod hanging by his side. The man looks up lazily and with a hint of arrogant defiance, but before recognition dawns, I spin my new shotgun around and smash the butt of it into the bridge of his nose, directly between his eyes.

Blood sprays across his face as his knees buckle and he topples onto his back, dropping the cattle prod as he does so. Before he can recover his senses, I hit him again, harder, until he lays still.

"Enough!" says Matylda.

With my fury still burning through me, I jab a finger at the group of huddled, half-naked women in the center of our melee. "Ask them if it's enough."

Matylda doesn't answer as I snatch up the cattle prod and slide it into my belt before stomping back to my position beside Berta. Her captive dropped his shotgun immediately after I laid out his friend. I pick it up by the strap and sling it over my shoulder.

"That was badass," whispers Berta as I stand beside her.

"You can practice on him," I whisper back, indicating her captive.

The man gulps and a stream of urine suddenly darkens his jeans. Instead of eliciting sympathy, it makes me hate him even more. A man so weak that he needs to kidnap and torture women to feel in charge.

"Who's the boss here?" the leader demands, his head swiveling between Matylda and myself. "Cause you're fucking with the wrong people."

"We want answers," says Matylda.

"To what? This is business, and it's not *your* fucking business."

Despite Matylda's warning to back off, I rush forward again— only this time with the cattle prod in my hand. A jolt of blue lightning melts his shirt against his skin, causing him to drop swiftly to one knee as I jab the prod into his side.

"Shut up and listen," I hiss. "Because I enjoy this shit."

"*Pierdol się, kurwa!*"

I stick him with the cattle prod again, dropping him to both hands and knees.

"I don't know what you just said," I seethe. "But I'm guessing it wasn't fucking polite."

Matylda moves forward and touches my arm. "We need him alive."

"Why? We have others."

The callous rebuttal has the desired effect as a look of genuine fear enters the man's stormy gray eyes. It's enough to make me step back and give Matylda the floor.

"A young woman died this morning," she tells the man, her voice desperately trying to hide its grief. "Somebody put a bomb inside her. We want to know who."

The man spits blood from a bit tongue as he pushes back onto his knees. "I don't know nothing about that."

I touch the cattle prod to the ground, causing a spark to jump between rocks.

"Okay, okay." The man holds up a hand to stop me from approaching. "It's not my crew. We're not into that. It's a waste of *pipka*."

"What's *pipka*?" I ask.

"Pussy," says Berta.

I bristle and slip the cattle prod back into my belt, leaving both hands free to handle the shotgun. I pump the action, allowing the noisy *click-clack* to punctuate my intention.

The man panics, his eyes growing larger as he reaches out to grab Matylda's leg.

"Touch her and I'll blow your fucking arm off," I warn.

"*Spierdalaj*, you make me nervous."

"Answer the question, then," I shout back. "And if you curse at me in Polish one more time, I'm going to shoot off a foot and then your dick."

The man holds up both hands. "I swear, I do not touch bombs."

"Who does?" asks Matylda, easing into her role of reasonable bitch versus my demonically-possessed-and-kinda-getting-off-on-it bitch.

The man hesitates, and this time Matylda holds out her hand to me. "Give me the thing."

I hand over the cattle prod and show her how the switch on top makes it spark.

"Okay, okay." The man squirms. "We sell some of our *kurwa—*" He glances over at me in terror. "Er, *merchandise* to others. We do not question what for, so long as they do not compete with us for the sex."

"You will give me names," says Matylda.

"Yes, yes, but—"

"No buts," I snarl. "Give her all the names or say goodbye to your nuts." I point an angry finger at the trembling and confused women still huddled together in the center of our fracas. "They look hungry enough to eat *anything*."

The man lowers his head, defeated.

Matylda turns to Julita and Krystyna. "Tie these *dupek* up. Tight. Then get the names from them." She then hands me a flashlight and says, "You and Berta make sure the container is empty. Irena will lead the first group of women to the van. We've been here too long."

"Wait a minute," protests the leader. "You're not taking all—"

Matylda silences him by jabbing the cattle prod into his chest and holding it there until he begins frothing pink foam at the mouth.

I flash an approving smile as I pass, and she surprises me with a discreet wink back.

———

The interior of the shipping container reeks of human filth. So much so that I want to pinch my nose and rush back outside to breathe.

"How could this possibly get past Customs?" I ask. "You can smell it's not engine parts."

"It is a game to them," says Berta. "They move the containers around like …" She struggles to find the right words. "Like Las Vegas shell game."

I shine a light into the darkest corners, noticing where the interior walls have been ripped open to expose narrow, vertical spaces just as Berta described. There are no holes in the false walls to provide light or air, which means every woman would have been trapped in the pitch black.

During the day, the bare metal container would have been an oven. At night, a freezer. I recall my conversation with Irena on our drive here when she said the ship had arrived two nights earlier.

I imagine being trapped in that cramped, dark space for even two days. I know I wouldn't be the same person coming out as I was going in.

My blood boils—then my flashlight catches the dull and mottled gray of sallow flesh.

Berta and I rush to the slumped woman's side, but I'm already sensing it's too late. Lying half-in and half-out of the vertical coffin, the woman's turbid eyes are open, but there is no movement in her chest.

I touch my fingers to her neck and feel for a pulse. Her flesh is cool to the touch.

"I can't feel anything," I say. "Do you have a mirror?"

Berta looks me as if I've asked for a rocketship to the moon, which considering our surroundings, I can't blame her. It's a stupid question, yet I feel the need to explain.

"If you hold a mirror beneath someone's nostrils, you can tell if they're breathing," I babble. "Sometimes a pulse can be so weak—"

Berta squeezes my arm and shakes her head. "I have seen many dead. She is gone."

I don't want to cry. I'm too angry for tears, but this woman is barely out of her teens. I stroke her face and brush a hand over her head, trying to fix the mess of her tangled hair, wishing there was something I could say—a prayer, an apology, anything.

This was someone's daughter.

"Let's look for others," says Berta, pulling me away. "It is not good to linger."

We find three more.

All young. All innocent. All dead.

Outside, Julita and Krystyna have tied the four men as though they are prize hogs being readied for slaughter. The first guard I hit still hasn't regained full consciousness and his head sits at an awkward angle, but after what I've seen, I don't feel the slightest bit of guilt.

Gerek, on the other hand, has opened his puffy blackening eyes and begun to look around. The thought of him stomping around the container, herding the women out like cattle while leaving the four dead ones behind to rot stabs a pain deep in my chest.

I rush forward in blind fury, slinging the shotgun off my shoulder to stab the barrel into his left eye.

"*Do kurwy nędzy!*" he yells.

"In English!" I snarl back.

"Why are you doing this?" he squeals.

"Because you disgust me."

"Who am I to you? I do not know you."

"I'm an avenging fucking angel, you prick."

Matylda moves beside me, worry on her brow. "You know this man?"

"Briefly. He pinched my ass once. I broke his finger."

"It would appear he is not smart, but is he worth a bullet?"

Without answering, I press the barrel deeper into his eye socket.

Gerek whimpers and the unmistakable smell of fresh shit creeps over him.

"We have to go," says Matylda. "Friends are sending a second van, but we must meet them now. If you must kill him, do it quickly and quietly. He is nothing to us."

As Gerek opens his mouth to protest, Julita moves in from behind to stuff a rag in his mouth. She wraps it in place with duct tape.

"I hate when they whine," she says with a wink, followed almost immediately by a wrinkle of her nose. "Phew! He's ripe."

Resisting the overpowering urge to pull the trigger, I remove the shotgun from his eye socket and step back. Matylda's right; unless I'm willing to take all four of the bastards down, Gerek's not worth the bullet.

"You OK?" Berta asks, reaching out to stroke my arm.

The other women are gathering up the weapons and a liberated money belt of cash that I assume was meant to be either an advance on wages or a payoff for the guards on the gate.

"What about the dead?" I ask.

Berta shakes her head and takes my hand, pulling me away from the horror and back to the gap in the fence.

Although I want to, neither of us looks back.

ELEVEN

AT THE VAN, I strip off the borrowed fatigues and toss them inside. I also unload both Mossberg shotguns before handing them to Julita to be packed away.

Matylda's eyes narrow with concern when I don't climb inside. "You are not coming with us?"

"I'll meet you tomorrow to go over those names," I say. "But I have another obligation first."

"Reporter stuff?" Matylda frowns and her voice becomes hard. "What will you write?"

"Don't worry, I'm not stupid enough to implicate myself or my new friends, but I can't leave four dead women back there. You've trusted me this far. That's not going to change."

Matylda gestures toward the stuffed interiors of the two vans. A dozen pairs of eyes in each. "And what of these women?"

"They're not tonight's story, they've been hurt enough. Tonight is about those who didn't make it."

Matylda's eyes soften slightly. "Be careful."

"You too. We'll talk tomorrow."

Matylda is the last to climb inside the packed van. As I swing the rear door closed, Berta leans forward to wave and offers a full smile with her eyes to make up for the half-smile on her lips.

———

After the vans disappear from sight, I pull out my new phone and tap in Frank's home number. He answers on the third ring.

"It's late," he grumbles.

"Sorry, but I have an anonymous tip."

"Dixie?"

"Didn't I just say it's anonymous?"

"I know your voice."

"Well forget it, this is anonymous."

A heavy sigh. "It's never just 'hello' with you, is it?"

"Hello."

He snorts and I can imagine his bones crackling as he stretches them awake.

"OK. Go."

I tell him about the four dead women in a shipping container.

"And how do you know this?" he asks.

"I received a tip."

"Uh-huh. And why do you believe—"

"They're here, Frank," I interrupt. "And unless you want me to kick down the front gate to the yard and create another Homeland Security alert—"

"OK. OK. For an anonymous caller, you sure remind me of a certain pain-in-the-balls reporter who—"

"I'll meet you at the front gate." I hang up.

———

It takes Frank close to half an hour to arrive at the yard's front gate with young Det. Russell Shaw at the wheel. While Frank looks like he's stumbled out of bed and sleepily yanked on the same clothes he left lying on the floor hours earlier, Shaw is impeccably dressed in off-duty jeans, T-shirt, and casual sport coat.

He flashes me a cute-but-too-eager smile—unlike Frank, whose grumpy visage is not remotely cute at all—as he climbs out of the car.

Frank holds up a piece of paper. "This warrant cost me a bottle of scotch and a favor that could have been put to better use, so I hope you're not jerking my chain, Dix."

"Wouldn't dream of it."

Two armed security guards step out of the guard booth as we approach. Neither of them looks particularly pleased to see us. After Frank shows them his badge and warrant, the older of the two returns to the booth to make a phone call to his superiors.

As we wait, I peer through the fence to the yard beyond, wondering how I'll explain the four trussed-up men, when I spot the first hints of smoke. It's rising from the same area where the traffickers were unloading their human cargo.

I turn to Shaw in panic. "It's on fire. They're burning the container."

Shaw darts over and peers through the darkness to where I'm pointing. The smoke is beginning to darken and bloom, but it's difficult to tell how engulfed it is in the foggy, moonless night.

"How do you know that's the same container you were told about?" he asks.

"What else would they set fire to?" I snap back.

Shaw quickly moves over to Frank and tells him of my fear. Frank nods and heads into the guard shack with a face that unnerves its occupant.

Within moments, the three of us are riding in the older guard's Jeep toward the rising smoke. The younger guard stays behind to call the fire department and monitor the gate.

The portable halogen work lights are still glowing around the container when we arrive, but there's no sign of the four trussed-up traffickers. Instead, the ground is littered with remnants of plastic zip ties and nylon cord, along with several small pools of congealing blood.

Shaw instantly grabs a small fire extinguisher from the back of the Jeep and sprays it into the fiery container. Despite his best efforts, however, the extinguisher doesn't contain enough foam to quell the blaze.

After the extinguisher runs dry, all we can do is stand back and watch as choking black smoke billows out of the container, destroying every last piece of evidence.

"What you thinking is in there?" asks the guard.

"Bodies," I say.

"Huh." The guard turns to Frank. "You think that, too?"

"If Dixie says it, I believe her."

"Huh." The guard turns back to me. "You got a tip? Who from?"

"It was anonymous."

"Man or woman?" he asks.

"Why do you care?"

"Just curious. Only two of us working patrol tonight and neither of us saw nothin' unusual."

"Then who started the fire?" I press back.

The guard shrugs. "It happens. Rats scurry round here, knock somethin' over, causes a spark and ... ain't unusual is all I'm sayin'. Probably oily engine parts in there, greasy rags, you know, flammable shit."

I tense at the approaching sound of a fire engine, its siren splitting the fog like a scalpel and making the filings in my teeth ache.

"It was rats alright." I stare hard at the guard, holding his gaze for an uncomfortable period of time. "The two-legged kind."

———

After the firemen knock down the blaze, the steaming interior of the shipping container looks like the inside of a coal furnace—black against black.

"Nothin' in there," says the guard, a hint of relief apparent in his voice.

"Help me with the lights," I say to Shaw.

Together we pick up the portable stands and move them closer to the container doors, aiming the light inside.

"It's still hot in there," cautions one of the firemen. "I wouldn't—"

"We think there were women inside. Four of them."

"Shit." He glances over at his men to make sure they have his back. "Stand back. We're dressed for it."

Slipping the plastic visor and oxygen mask back over his ruggedly handsome face, the fireman picks up his pole—a long, red crowbar with a forked tip—and wades into the mess.

"They were against the walls," I shout after him, which earns me a questioning look from Frank.

After a few minutes of smashing about, the fireman returns, his face a darker ash than before. He looks past me to catch Frank's eye and nods.

"They're still in there?" I ask, already knowing the answer.

"I don't want to destroy the scene any further," he answers with a heavy voice. "But I saw enough."

When I turn to Frank, he's already on the phone, calling in a forensic team.

"Thanks," I say to the fireman. "Sorry to ruin your night."

He fixes me with a troubled stare. "Did you know them?"

"No, but it's important they were found."

"Sometimes…" He shakes his head, stopping himself from putting words to his thoughts, and I wonder if he recognizes me as a reporter. He changes direction instead. "You take care now."

"You too," I say as he returns to his men to pack up their gear. "And thank you."

Soon the scene is flooded with forensic specialists and I'm simply getting in the way.

"I'm going to file the story and head home," I tell Frank. "Can I call you from the office to confirm the number of dead?"

"You already know."

"I know how many are supposed to be inside, but I need the official count for the story."

Frank sighs wearily. "We won't be talking to the media until later in the day. You know they'll all be wanting to tie this in with the bombing, and until I know a hell of a lot more—"

"I just want a number," I interrupt, squeezing his arm in an attempt to temper his darkening mood. "We'll deal with the rest tomorrow."

"And what is the rest?" Frank presses.

"I know as much as you do."

"Somehow I doubt that."

"If I knew more, I'd tell you."

"Would you?"

"You know I would."

Frank shrugs. "I used to believe that." He points down at the trampled spatters of blood and discarded plastic ties. "Somebody knows what the fuck happened here."

I lift up on my tiptoes to meet his fatigued gaze and squeeze his arm harder. "If I get a name, it's yours. I promise."

Some of the heat leaves Frank's face, but not all. "I'll hold you to that."

Before leaving the scene, I move into the shadows and use what I learned in the afternoon tech session to bring up the smartphone's camera app. The portable lights cast enough of a devilish glow to make the crime scene eerie and disturbing.

———

At the deserted *NOW* offices, I upload one of the gloomy photos and a short story headlined: *Four women dead in shipyard.* I don't have enough detail for a print story—names, suspects, origin and/or owner of the container, official cause of death, etc.—but in this day of digital first, I'm hoping beating the competition may earn me some much-needed Brownie points with the publisher.

When I'm done, I leave a note for Stoogan explaining the follow-up that needs to be assigned in the morning since I may get in late.

Then I wait, my finger hovering over the enter key, until my phone beeps with the confirmation I need.

Frank's text message is short and to the point: *Four.*

I hit enter and call Mo's for a taxi.

TWELVE

A LOUD POP STARTLES me awake as Prince rushes into the room with his tail puffed out and standing straight in the air. After leaping on the bed, he rushes toward me to make sure I'm awake and have his back before digging in his claws to spin around. Facing the doorway, he arches his spine and hisses at whatever has frightened him.

Grabbing my phone off the nightstand, I tap in the first two numbers for 911 and wait.

Nothing happens. The apartment is completely silent.

With an exhalation of relief, I gently stroke Prince's fur and ask, "What did you do?"

It takes awhile before he finds his purr, but soon his fur settles back to normal and his tail relaxes. I try to think what he could have possibly got into to make that popping sound but come up blank.

Finally, curiosity gets the better of me and I climb out of bed, slip into my Godzilla slippers, and investigate.

Lying on the floor near the couch, I find a bright yellow patch of rubber that appears to be the burst skin of a balloon. Stretching the rubber in my hands, I see that it's decorated with an iconic smiley face.

Tied to the nub of the balloon is a small white ribbon. Written on the ribbon in heavy felt marker is the single word: *Hello*. Except the *o* has been replaced with a circle of solid red.

I turn to see Prince hesitating by the bedroom door, waiting to make sure the coast is clear.

"Don't blame you," I tell him. "Happy faces are spooky."

With no idea where it came from, I carry the dead balloon into the kitchen and toss it in the trash. Since I'm up, I pour breakfast for Prince and plug in the coffeemaker.

Yawning, I study the hastily scrawled note that I stuck to the fridge door last night. It reads: *New Phone Number*, followed by my new phone number. I recite the number a few times, looking for a pattern to make it easier. Not that I'm actually planning to give it to anyone, but if, for example, a cute fireman needed to get in touch, I'd hate to blow the moment by being the bumbling idiot who doesn't know her own cell number.

The moment boiling water hits the coffee grounds, there's a knock followed by Kristy's singsong voice: "Hey, Dix. You home?"

I hear her trying the door, but it's been made impenetrable by a custom four-way deadbolt system from a local security company that specializes in panic rooms. At least I wasn't so tired when I got home last night that I forgot to be paranoid.

Dixie's Tips #25: *They say being paranoid doesn't mean some-one is out to get you, but neither does it mean someone isn't—and*

I have the scars to prove it. Besides, one more violent incident in my apartment and Mrs. Pennell may ask me to leave. I only hope the door is tax-deductible because the cost was painful.

"I'm coming," I call.

On a discreet panel beside the door, I punch in the security code to release the deadbolts with a satisfying clunk and open up. Kristy is beaming as she excitedly holds up two brown paper bags.

"Guess what I bought?" she asks.

"Smiley face balloons?"

Kristy frowns. "No. Where'd that come from?" She shakes her head dismissively, then rattles the first bag. "Fresh bagels, still warm." She rattles the second bag. "And two kinds of cream cheese, one with lox already mixed in."

My stomach growls with interest, which makes Kristy's smile grow even larger. "Thought you'd like that."

As Kristy enters, I look behind her for Sam.

"Sam's training today," Kristy explains. "Early start."

"Training for what?" I lead the way to the kitchen and pull out two plates for the bagels and two mugs for coffee.

"To be a trainer. Guess she's so good at her job, her bosses want her to train new recruits."

Sam is employed by the SFMTA, or San Francisco Municipal Transportation Agency.

"That's cool."

"Yeah," Kristy agrees. "Once she starts, it'll mean regular hours and no more shift work."

"That'll be great for both of you."

"I know," Kristy beams. "Especially when—" She hesitates.

"Especially when *what*?" I press.

Kristy wrinkles her nose. "I can't say. Not yet." But the excited glow on her face lets the secret out.

"You're pregnant?" I ask.

Kristy winces. "I haven't had the test yet. Sam and I always go together, but—" She covers her mouth to suppress a giggle. "It feels like, maybe."

Rushing over, I envelope her in a big hug. "That's wonderful."

She giggles again and squeezes me back. "Don't tell Sam I said anything, will you? We're going to the appointment together tomorrow morning."

I release her and turn an imaginary key in an imaginary lock across my lips.

"Now let's eat," I say. "I'm starved."

———

After breakfast, I shower, dress, and head down to the lobby. The day's mail hasn't arrived yet, so I put any thoughts about suspicious red packages and an unsettling game of hangman out of my head. Instead, I knock on Mr. French's door.

I hear him telling his pet parakeet, Baccarat, to preen her feathers for company. And when he opens the door, his face lights up as though I am the best surprise possible.

"Miss Flynn, how wonderful. You arrived home so late last night that I was worried you wouldn't be allowed to catch up on your sleep. But here you are, looking all bright eyed and bushy tailed."

I laugh. "I don't know if I would go that far. Can I come in for a moment?"

"Of course, of course." Mr. French steps aside to allow me entrance. "Where are my manners? Baccarat would give me such a scolding if I didn't allow her to say hello. Can I offer you breakfast tea?"

"No, I'm fine, thanks. Kristy and I had coffee."

"Delightful. Such a lovely girl, Kristy, and practically glowing these days too. I wonder if she's using a new face scrub? I must remember to ask."

In the cramped living room filled with Mr. French's eclectic bric-a-brac, I settle on the mahogany Queen Anne loveseat facing his favorite armchair.

Once settled, Mr. French studies my face and says, "You're looking very serious, Miss Flynn. Is this about your mysterious packages? I'm afraid that I haven't been able to find anything out yet, but—"

"It's not that," I interrupt. "I need to locate someone and was hoping I could call on your services. I know where he usually hangs out, so it's a matter of watching and waiting, but it's in a bad part of town." I wince. "Actually, a *really* bad part of town."

Intrigued, Mr. French leans forward. "And what do you need with this person?"

"The bodies of four women were discovered in a shipping container last night. This man works for the people responsible, and I need to know who they are."

"And you believe this individual will talk to you?"

"If I get him alone, he'll tell me everything."

Mr. French rubs his hands together in gleeful anticipation. "Where is his hangout?"

"The Sandford Hotel. He frequents the bar there."

"Ah, I know it." His eyes twinkle. "There are several rather unsavory lodging houses surrounding the premises that are easily rented by the day. I'm sure I could find one that offers a suitable vantage point. I can set up in one of the rooms and be both invisible and perfectly comfortable."

"Are you sure?" I ask.

A smile brightens his face. "Oh, I'm more than sure, Miss Flynn. I would be insulted if you had asked any other. It will also give me the perfect opportunity to use my new Swarovski birding scope. When would you like me to set up?"

"As soon as possible."

He jumps to his feet. "Right then, to action. Tell me all about this horrid man while I prepare a thermos and sandwiches. I should give Clifford a call for an extra set of eyes. He's been dying for another adventure, and we can discuss your red wrapping paper at the same time."

Baccarat chirps loudly at all the commotion as Mr. French gets busy.

THIRTEEN

Through the street-level kitchen window, I spot my taxi pulling up as Mr. French pours boiling water into a matching pair of stainless-steel thermoses.

"Remember," I caution as I head out, "observation only. This creep is dangerous. Call when you spot him."

Mr. French puts on a mock serious face and salutes, which makes me burst into laughter. His platinum mustache and gloriously bright eyes remind me of the sergeant on an old British sitcom that used to run on PBS and was a cheesy favorite of my father's.

Inside the cab, I dig out my phone and notice that it's still in silent mode from the night before—and that I've missed several phone calls. I return Frank's call first.

"I need you to come to the station," he says without preamble.

"When?"

"Now is good."

"You just can't start your day without seeing my smiling face, can you? Face it, Frank, I'm the caffeine in your coffee, the sugar on your doughnut, the vitamin D in your sun—"

"The pain in my ass," he finishes dryly.

"Always the charmer." I turn serious. "One question: Am I in trouble?"

"When aren't you?"

"True, but you know what I mean. Last night?"

"You're not in trouble. You got a tip, you told me, we're good."

"And I'm working on getting a name for you."

"Uh-huh. How?"

"I know someone who may know someone who may know something."

"I'll hold my breath, then."

Ignoring his sarcasm, I add, "Plus, I'm seeing Ania's aunt today and I've told her you want to talk. She's not very trusting of police, but I've told her you're not as big a jerk as most."

"Charming."

"Hey, I'm being sincere here."

"That's the scary part."

My next call is to my editor.

"Am I great or what?" I ask when Stoogan answers. "Photo and story on our site before the competition even opened its eyes. Betcha some poor schmo is getting his ass chewed this morning while you're puckering up to kiss mine."

"Who the hell is this?" Stoogan barks, catching me off guard.

"Seriously?"

He chuckles, enjoying his own joke. "Don't get a big head, Dix."

"But?"

"But?" He's confused.

"'But good job' is what you're supposed to say."

"Yeah, OK, good job," he concedes. "I wasn't aware you even knew how to upload your own stuff."

"Nobody else was around. It read okay?"

"Not bad. Light on the facts and a small typo in the cutline, but we caught it first thing. I've assigned John to the follow unless you're planning to take it. Lot of unanswered questions."

"I'm sticking with the bombing for now, but there's definitely a deeper story here that I'm going to want to explore."

"You think the two are connected?"

"We'll see. I'm on my way to the cops now to dig a little deeper."

"One question, cause the publisher is bound to ask: How were you the only media on scene? I'm hearing chatter there was no mention of bodies being found in that crate until *after* your story went live."

"Charm, intellect, and beauty, boss. My usual trifecta."

"Hmmm, if you say so. But be careful out there; your knack for finding trouble scares me sometimes."

"Don't let the newsroom hear you say that, boss. They might suspect you have a heart."

Stoogan hangs up before I can.

———

At the Hall of Justice—an imposing granite mausoleum that houses police headquarters, the district attorney's office, courtrooms, and two county jails—I make my way to the front desk and have them call Frank.

He appears at the bank of elevators a few minutes later and gestures for me to join him.

"So what's up?" I ask.

"Need to show you something."

"Cryptic."

The tiniest flicker of a smile—either that or he's got gas.

"We've been poring over video from yesterday. Everybody and their dogs are shooting video these days, so it's a massive job, but it helps us piece together things surveillance cameras don't always catch."

"Such as?" I probe.

"I'll show you, but I need a promise first."

"Sounds dodgy."

He ignores me. "People are questioning the access you have to sensitive police information. Revealing the bomber's name yesterday, and then your report on the four dead women this morning. I was hauled into the chief's office—"

"You didn't give me either of those," I protest.

"That's what I told the chief, but it still doesn't look good. When you were sticking to your investigative pieces, there wasn't a problem. Your tenacity may piss people off, but at least they understood it when they read your work. This instant-Internet crap, however, is making everybody nervous."

"Let me guess, the media barons drink at the same club as the mayor and they're pissed because little ol' me is showing up their overpaid talking heads."

"No comment." He pauses briefly to switch gears. "I'd value your opinion, but I don't want anything broadcast on your website about what you see. Agreed?"

I shrug half-heartedly. "I'll go along, except I retain the right to use the information in print if I feel it's important to the story."

Frank offers a half-nod. "You're a good writer, Dix, and you've never screwed me in print. That's why I trust you."

"Plus, I'm cute," I rally back cheekily.

Frank's lips curl upwards. "I'm not sure that's the first word that comes to mind."

"Too self-deprecating?" I ask. "Should I have gone with gorgeous, stunning, *superfabulabulous*—"

The elevator doors open before Frank can offer a rebuttal.

———

Frank leads me through an open squad room filled with a scattering of plainclothes and uniforms working behind old-school desks and last-generation computers to a set of oversized, frosted-glass doors. Behind the doors is a more streamlined, less paper-hungry room stuffed with nerd cops on high-end computers and ergonomic chairs.

Overly ambitious air-conditioning is battling a recent bulk sale on short-sleeved shirts to make a landscape of goosebumps rise on skinny arms that look liable to buckle at the recoil of a department-issue SIG Sauer P229.

"This must be where you hide all the cool kids," I say aloud.

Several heads glance up from their monitors to smile at me with flossed appreciation.

Dixie's Tips #26: *Pointing out irony doesn't always endear one to others. Sometimes it's best to pretend you're actually being sincere.*

"We call it the Geek Squad," says Frank. "But more and more it's becoming the hub of good police work. You'd be surprised what killers, thieves, dealers, pedophiles, and rapists post on the web. Robbery division took down a theft ring last week by linking an eBay profile to a Tumblr account where the clowns posted photos of themselves wearing the same masks used in a string of robberies."

"That's why I'm not on Facebook," I say.

"Because you're a thief?" Pipes up one of the cops—a youthful blonde with seriously deep dimples in both cheeks.

"Only of hearts," I quip back. "Don't want all those spurned lovers tracking me down. I'm sure you can relate."

The cop blushes slightly and returns to his computer as Frank rolls his eyes. He leads me to a computer being operated by a caramel-skinned cop with a close-cropped, inky scalp and sensual eyes. He introduces us, but the lack of pupil response tells me I'm not his type. It happens.

"Emilio noticed something off in one of the videos we downloaded from a witness's phone," Frank explains. "He then matched it with other videos to compile a more complete picture." He taps Emilio on the shoulder. "Play it."

Emilio plays the linked clips. It's a bit like watching one of those low budget, found-footage horror movies, except the cameraman is jonesing for Adderall.

"What do you see?" asks Frank.

I reach over Emilio's shoulder and indicate the face of a man on the edge of the frame watching Ania fall to her death from the top of the parking structure.

"Everyone else is horrified," I say. "But he looks angry."

Emilio smiles. "Good eye, but there's more."

With the click of his mouse, Emilio zooms in, not on the man's face, but on his hands.

I strain forward for a closer look, but the image is blurry. "What's he holding?" I ask.

"We think it's a remote device for the bomb," says Frank.

I snap back. "Really?"

"I'll play it again," says Emilio, "but this time watch his hands."

I watch the video again and feel anger rising in my chest. There's a twitch of his thumb a split-second before the explosion.

"One more time," I say.

I study the man's hands and face, piecing it together: his thumb hovering over the button of a small, electronic device; his face triumphant, almost gleeful before turning to anger in the moment the camera sweeps up to catch Ania plunging to her death.

"He didn't expect Ania to jump," I say, turning to Frank. "So what was his plan?"

"That's what we're still trying to figure out."

My brain is churning at a thousand thoughts per minute. "Where would you have taken Ania if we had talked her off the edge? Here?"

"No." Frank's eyes narrow in concentration. "Straight to a hospital. She presented as pregnant and suicidal. I would have wanted a doctor to make sure the baby was okay before dealing with her mental state."

I feel the blood drain from my face. "Can you imagine if that was his plan? To get a bomb inside the maternity ward?" My thoughts continue to churn as the horrific scenario playing in my brain makes me weak at the knees. "And by being brought in by the police, she would have been rushed straight through. No arguing with nurses about doctors or insurance. If Ania hadn't jumped …"

"You have a dark imagination," says Frank. "I hadn't considered that angle."

"Look at his face," I say. "He's pleased when Ania is talking to us but angry when she jumps. Either he meant to target us on the roof or he wanted her escorted elsewhere. From his vantage point on the street, he wouldn't be able to tell how many cops, if any, were near enough to be caught in the blast. So I'm betting the latter."

Frank turns to Emilio. "Bring up the composite."

With the click of a few buttons, Emilio displays a photo composite of the suspect on the screen.

"This is what I was able to piece together from the various bits of footage. None of the angles gave us a clear, front-on view, so some of it is guesswork."

I lean forward again to study the face. He has the angular, flat look of an electric iron: wide forehead and high cheekbones; sharp, beak-like nose; narrow, jutting chin with wisps of white, almost transparent whiskers dangling from it like errant spider silk; a significant, oddly-shaped stain or birthmark on his left cheek; and a series of stainless-steel piercings in his left ear. The right side of his face is less detailed, which tells me there wasn't enough footage of that side to be more specific. Unfortunately, his eyes are hidden behind sunglasses, and a baseball hat covers most of his hair.

"I thought you were interviewing witnesses on the street?" I say.

"We interviewed everybody who stuck around, but we weren't expecting a bomb so it took awhile to get the area locked down." Frank points at the screen. "He didn't linger. We've run the face through our data banks, but no hits yet. He look familiar?"

The tone in Frank's voice irks me. "And what makes you think that's a possibility?" I ask.

"You've been hanging in some dark corners of the city lately. Your paths could've crossed."

I shake off the suggestion. "Never seem him before."

"You sure?"

"Positive." My gaze hardens. "If I had, I'd give him up in a heartbeat. That's a face I'd remember."

"Worth a shot," he says, his tone relaxing. "I've run it past Narcotics and Vice, but none of them recognize him either, which tells me he must be relatively new to town."

"Why attract this much attention to himself?" I ask. "Bombing a maternity ward would put him on every watch list in the country."

"If he was planning to take credit, sure," admits Frank. "But apart from a few overly curious fathers, nobody shoots video at hospital. If Ania hadn't jumped, we wouldn't have his face."

The thought makes me sick. I point at the disturbing composite on the screen. "Can I get a print-out?"

Frank hesitates. "One condition: You keep it to yourself until the brass decides it's time to go public."

"Sure, but I would think you want as many people looking for this creep as possible."

"That's not my call."

"Bosses, huh? Pain in the ass for everyone."

"No comment."

FOURTEEN

BACK ON THE STREET, I call Dr. Irena Krawiec to see if I can connect with Ania's aunt to go over the list of names we retrieved from the traffickers.

"It's Dixie," I say when she answers. "Everyone okay?"

"*Tak*, everyone is fine, but I see no mention of arrests in your story this morning."

"There was nobody there to arrest. Somehow they got free, set fire to the container, and fled before I could bring the police."

"That is unfortunate."

"You worried there will be repercussions?"

"There are always repercussions."

I wince. "We should have worn masks."

"Bah! A group of angry Polish women are not so easily disguised. We know the risks, no?"

"I'm not Polish," I say.

Irena chuckles. "You are one of us now."

"Hmmm, maybe, but just for the record, I'm still not eating borscht."

Irena chuckles again. "You wish to go over names? Same building as last night. One hour."

"I'll be there."

———

After the taxi drops me off, I press my nose against the bakery window and inhale before heading inside. Everything looks and smells incredible, but I limit myself to a dozen traditional *paczki* stuffed with a variety of fruit and creme fillings, including *powidła* (stewed plum jam), wild rose hip jam, Bavarian cream, custard, raspberry, and apple.

With my box of powdered goodies in hand, I enter the nearby alley and stop in the shadow of a commercial dumpster with a large sticker on the side that reads: *Cardboard Only*.

Leaning against the brick wall, I wait in the dank darkness with only the wafting aroma of the sweet treats and my not-so-sweet imagination for company.

After five minutes of undisturbed solitude, I decide I'm not being followed by vengeful sex traffickers. Slipping my knife from below the box of goodies, I return it to its sheath in my boot before continuing to the narrower offshoot and the rusted steel door at its terminus. I knock twice.

When the door opens, Berta pops her head out and squeals in delight before grabbing me in a lung-collapsing hug. Fortunately, I'm fast enough to whip the box of doughnuts out to the side before it's crushed along with my ribs.

"You had me worried," gushes Berta. "Staying behind like that with those men so angry."

"I called the cops for backup before I went in," I say with a smile. "I'm hot-headed but not stupid."

Berta releases me from her death-grip hug and pulls me inside. "They get away, I hear."

I nod. "Somebody untied them, then set a fire to cover their tracks."

"Men like that stay angry for long, long time. We need to be careful and watch backs."

I show her the white box. "I brought *paczki* to keep our energy up."

Berta smiles as wide as she can without hurting the burnt side of her face. "*Powidła* is my favorite."

"Then that one is yours."

When we enter the sparse room, Matylda and Irena are already inside, their faces flushed from a heated and abruptly ended conversation. I place the bakery box on a table in front of them and flip open the lid to release an aroma impossible to resist.

"Dig in," I say, "before the others get here."

Irena eyes the treats carefully, while Berta snatches up the one that looks most likely to have plum jam inside. Matylda, however, doesn't even glance down.

"The others are busy," she tells me, "settling the women and contacting their families if there are any."

"More for us then." I pluck out a doughnut and take a bite. It's exactly as good as dough, fat, and sugar can be.

Matylda hesitates before picking up one of the doughnuts and taking a small, tentative bite as though simply trying to be polite. I proceed to stuff the remainder of the fried dough in my mouth and chew with gusto before rubbing my hands together to remove the grease and powdered sugar.

"Did you look over the names?" I ask, my mouth still half-full, sensing her impatience.

Matylda nods, but it's brusque, like an axe on kindling.

"Any of them stand out?" I continue, wondering if I should ask what's wrong.

"Not so much, but I do not know most of people in this line of work." She hands me a folded piece of paper. "I make you copy."

Before I open the paper, I have to ask: "Are you pissed at me?"

Matylda glances over at Irena before exhaling loudly. "Large ox in room."

I'm confused until I realize she means elephant. "Yes," I say, "large ox."

Matylda folds her arms across her bosom and sighs again, pausing slightly to gather her words. "Your actions last night give me much to process," she begins. "Your anger frightens me and I was shamed, but when Irena and I talk today I realize it is not you that cause upset, it is me."

"I don't understand. You did great."

"I hesitate when I should not," she says, her voice pained. "These men are vipers, but only you saw their fangs. I—" A sad smile breaks on her lips. "I have always been woman of mind, of talk, but one cannot talk with gun pointed at head. If you had not acted, we could have been overpowered and killed. These men do not see us as

119

human. We are cargo, *prostytutka*, whores. Leaving them alive was foolish."

"You're not a killer," I say. "That's not a shameful thing."

"Blood is on my hands. I believed it could be washed away by doing good." She pinches the skin between her eyes. "It cannot. Blood once spilled must flow."

"I don't believe that," I say gently. "We needed to immobilize those men, which we did, but getting them arrested would be better than killing them. We don't need to start a gang war, especially since we don't have much of a gang. Those four got away last night, but that doesn't mean they got away forever. I'm trying to track one of them down now, but if you know any of the others or how I could locate them, please tell me."

"Sorry." Matylda shakes her head. "This is new to us, too. I turned blind eye until it is my own flesh involved."

Irena reaches over to squeeze her friend's shoulder, which looks as supple as rock, as I unfold the sheet of paper. There are six names written on it, but one is already crossed out.

"Who's this?" I ask, indicating the spoiled name.

Matylda glances over at Irena nervously before answering. "He is who I pay to bring Ania over from Poland. I talk with him after Ania disappeared, but he is foolish man with no answers. He claim Ania stolen before he can deliver her. He has no names to offer."

"But you didn't know about the bomb until yesterday," I press. "We should question him again in case he knows of some—"

Matylda cuts me off. "We cannot. It is not possible." The flash of pain and anger in her eyes tells me I've found the source of the blood on her hands. Whoever the man was, he's not talking to anyone ever again.

"What about associates?" I ask, changing tactics. "He must have worked with others."

"I did not know, but you are right." She looks down at her fingers, twisting together like a nest of nervous snakes. "These men do not work alone. I should have looked harder."

I rattle the paper. "There are five other names on here. Can you help me track them down?"

Matylda nods. "If they have connections with our community, we will uncover them, but we have to move with extra caution. Your—*our*—actions last night have stirred the nest. They may find us instead."

"Have there been threats?" I ask.

"Not yet, but—"

"Let them come," snarls Berta, her balled fist landing on the table top hard enough to make the *paczki* jump. "*Matkojebca* say we are whores, but we are fighters, and we will cut off their balls and feed to their children."

Matylda, Irena, and I stare at each other in shocked silence for a second before I recover and quip, "OK, that's enough sugar for you, sweetie."

Berta's face drops in disappointment until she notices the three of us are smiling with great affection. With a grunt, she snatches up another doughnut, tears it in half, and stuffs it in her mouth.

She can barely get it down before joining us in laughter.

After the laughter subsides, I pull out the composite photo that Frank's Geek Squad mocked up and lay it flat on the table.

"Does this face ring any bells?" I ask.

"Ring bells?" asks Berta, confused.

"Look familiar," I explain. "He was in the crowd when Ania died."

Matylda lifts up the photo and studies it in detail. "I do not know him," she says, "but he has a face difficult to hide." She focuses on me. "Why do you single him out?"

"The police can't be sure, but in video recovered from witnesses, he appears to be holding what could be a remote detonator for the bomb inside Ania."

Matylda's eyes grow hard. "You use a lot of uncertain words. *Can't be sure, appears to be, could be.*"

"That's the journalist in me, I guess. He's a lead, just like the names we recovered last night, but I don't have any proof he's responsible for Ania's death. The evidence is circumstantial at best, but he's acting highly suspicious in the footage I've seen."

"Will the police release this face?" Irena asks as she takes the photo from Matylda.

"Eventually. If they think it'll help."

"But in the meantime, we have head start?" she adds.

I offer a smile. "That's one way to look at it."

Irena and Matylda share a look. "We will put out word, see what rocks turn over."

I pluck a second doughnut from the box to nibble along its caramelized edge. "If you find him, let me know straight away. I have a few questions of my own to ask before we turn him over."

FIFTEEN

On the taxi ride over to Mario's Deli, my new cellphone rings and a number appears on its screen that I don't recognize.

I answer tentatively. "Hello?"

"Ah, Miss Flynn, it is you. Good."

"Mr. French?"

"At your service."

"I didn't know you owned a cellphone."

"I don't, or rather I didn't, but I thought for this adventure I would acquire a burner."

"A burner?" I say, surprised.

"Yes. Did you know they sell them at the corner store? I was under the illusion that I was going to have to negotiate with some unsavory chaps at a striptease club, but all I did was pop into 7-Eleven. Rather less exciting, I must admit. And I was told if one doesn't want to 'burn' it, you can even purchase extra minutes. Pity, really. I was rather hoping it self-destructed after a certain time or when you punched in an emergency code."

As I try to keep the laughter out of my voice, a troubling thought worms its way to the surface. "I forgot to give you my number, didn't I? How stupid is that?"

"Luckily, I am a detective."

"Uh-huh. Spill. How did you get this number?"

I can hear the sheepish smile in his voice. "I asked Kristy, actually. It wasn't until after you left that I realized we hadn't discussed a proper channel of communication. Fortunately, Kristy said you left a rather large note on your fridge with this number on it. Her opinion was it either had to be yours or belong to some secret gentleman you've been hiding under the stairs. But since I haven't seen any men recently, apart from that rather tough-looking Pinch fellow who likes to court on the doorstep—"

"OK," I interrupt, not wanting to hear a rundown of my pathetic love life. "Congratulations, it's my number. Now what's up?"

"Ahh, right. Good news. Clifford and I have spotted your man entering the hotel bar. He is looking disturbingly tousled with a bandaged nose and two black eyes. The left one is particularly bad. If he was to enter a costume contest as Quasimodo, I believe he would take home the blue ribbon. The swelling has all the appearance of an engorged purple plum."

"That's Gerek," I say. "Keep watch and let me know as soon as he leaves. I may need you to follow him until I get there, but remember not to get too close. He's dangerous."

"He certainly looks it," agrees Mr. French. "He was chewing a large onion as he limped up the street, so I dare say his breath alone could be a chemical weapon."

"An onion?"

"Yes, quite. He tossed it aside before entering the bar, but it was definitely an onion. I'm thinking one of the sweeter varieties, such as Walla Walla or Vidalia. I could retrieve it if you like and—"

"That's OK," I interrupt with a chuckle. "It's him I'm interested in, not his choice of snack."

"Understood, Miss Flynn. We have eyes on the door."

The taxi pulls up in front of Mario's Deli as I hang up.

———

When I enter the deli, Mario beams as though he hasn't seen me in weeks.

"Ms. Dixie," he calls. "You look hungry."

I laugh and pat my stomach. "Just coffee, thanks. I've been eating *paczki* with friends."

"Sugar is no good, you need protein to stay healthy. I have some beautiful smoked meat from Montreal that I lather with a grainy mustard and—"

"Maybe later," I interrupt. "Just coffee for now."

Mario's smile dims only slightly. "I'll bring it over."

Eddie the Wolf glowers at me from under his cap as I slide into the red vinyl booth to sit across from him. I'm used to his crankiness, but this look is more surly than most.

"What?" I ask.

"You Irish?"

"On my father's side. Why?"

"They say the Irish are lucky, but I've never known that to be the case—until now."

"I have no idea what you're talking about."

Eddie reaches into his pocket and slides an envelope across the table. I pick it up and look inside. It's lined with twenties; ten of them.

"Your dog came in."

I think back to the bet I placed yesterday. "Marmalade Spice?"

"Came from behind and nosed in for third place, which surprised the hell out of everybody, including the damn dog."

"But I bet to win."

"Yeah, stupid bet until the first two dogs were disqualified over some irregularities at the starting line. End result? Marmalade Spice took his first win. Ever."

I slide the money into my pocket with a large, cat-got-the-cream grin on my face as Mario walks over and places a coffee in front of me.

"You maybe want a sandwich to go?" he asks in a tone of concern. "You'll be hungry soon. Sugar burns up so quick."

With a chuckle I nod in agreement, which brings a return of the high beam to Mario's smile. He scuttles back behind the counter with a joyful bounce.

"So you come to rob me again?" Eddie asks. "Another long shot to pry money from my hand?"

"Actually, I'm wondering if I can chat with Jakub?"

Eddie's brow furrows, the dark valleys as deep as his eyes are hard.

"He asked me to look into something," I add before he can answer. "But I don't want to go behind your back. That's why I'm here. Talking to you first."

The valleys soften slightly. "Those four women you wrote about this morning. They connected to this?"

"That's part of it."

"They catch who did that?"

"Not yet, but I'm working on it."

Eddie's lips curl into something resembling a smile. "*You're* working on it?"

I shrug. "The cops are too, but maybe I can help get them there a little faster."

Eddie cups his hands as if weighing something heavy. "If I had a son, I'd want him to have your balls."

I can't help laughing. "I hope that's a compliment."

Eddie shrugs. "It is what it is."

"So can I talk with Jakub?"

Eddie scratches his nose, then digs in his jacket pocket to retrieve a crumpled ten-dollar bill. It's my original stake on the dogs. He holds it out to me. "Mario has your sandwich ready. Maybe you want to eat it round back."

I indicate the door behind him. "Through there?"

He shakes his head.

I stab my thumb at the street entrance behind me.

Eddie nods.

After sliding out of the booth, I pick up my sandwich—oozing warmth and wrapped snug in wax paper—and exit the deli. On the street, I drop the sandwich into my pocket and move to the alley that leads behind the building.

———

Jakub is sitting in his usual spot on the short wall behind the deli with a cigarette between his lips. He doesn't appear quite as imposingly gigantic as I remember from our first meeting, but he still looms large enough to make me think he's the Hulk to my Bruce Banner. If Bruce Banner was a sexy redhead, naturally.

"I hear you and my *ciotka* have been busy," he says as smoke flows from his nostrils.

"She's been showing me the sights."

Jakub's lips ripple and expose a flash of teeth. "She says you know how to fight."

"I've been learning a few things."

An eyebrow arches. "Someone is teaching you?"

"A girl's gotta look out for herself."

"The cop?" he asks. "Your friend."

This time I show some teeth, but it's not all friendly. I'm not big on being spied upon. "Among others."

Jakub takes the hint and shrugs. "Like you say. Best to be safe."

I pull out a piece of paper, but Jakub holds up a hand to stop me. "I have already seen the names. I will help where I can, but that is a different world and those men are not familiar to me. Eddie is a businessman, but he sticks to gambling. No drugs. No smuggling. No whores."

"You move in different circles," I say with only a touch of cynicism.

Jakub shows me his teeth again. "Exactly."

I unfold the piece of paper to show it doesn't contain a list of names, but rather a composite photo. I hand it over.

"Just in case your circles ever accidentally overlap, I'm wondering if you've come across this face?"

Jakub studies it carefully before looking up. "Who is this?"

"We think he may be the one who triggered the bomb inside Ania, the young Polish girl who was killed yesterday."

A low growl rumbles in the large man's throat. "It's not a face I recognize. You think he's Polish?"

"I couldn't even guess. The man who smuggled Ania into the country claimed she was stolen from him, but unfortunately he's no longer around for me to do any follow-up."

"Stolen?"

"From the docks during unloading. There have been reports of other women disappearing too. Perfect crime, really. All the women are already illegal, so who are the smugglers going to complain to?"

"If this is true, he"—Jakub stabs the photo—"will have a price on his head. Red Swan, among a few others, controls all smuggling. If he does not have a price tag, then that tells you something else."

My eyes burn with eagerness. "Could you find out?"

Jakub shrugs and nods.

"How long will—" My phone rings before I can finish the question. I recognize the number. "Is it okay if I take this?"

Jakub shrugs again and digs in his pocket for a fresh cigarette. He lights it off the stub of his old one.

"Mr. French," I say. "What have you got?"

"Ah, Miss Flynn. Your man has left the bar and is returning from whence he came, which appears to be an apartment complex of rather low bearing and shady repute."

"You're following him?"

"Do not fear, I have kept a safe distance. The man is oblivious to the tail thanks to Clifford, who is monitoring from the rooftops and feeding me precise directions."

"Is he with anyone?"

"No, he's quite alone. Ah, he's entering the building now. I have the address."

"Stay outside. I'm on my way. And Mr. French ..."

"Yes?"

"Brilliant work."

"A pleasure as always, Miss Flynn."

After I get the address, I turn to Jakub and ask, "Would Eddie mind if I borrowed you for half an hour?"

A lone eyebrow arches behind the drifting cigarette smoke. "Why?"

"The four Polish women who died on the docks last night."

His eyes harden. "Yeah?"

"I've found one of the bastards responsible and I want him to tell me who else was involved and who's running the show."

"And?"

"He's frightened of me, but I'm betting you'll terrify him."

Jakub flashes a set of teeth that reminds me of a hungry, hungry hippo approaching a Las Vegas buffet.

"I'm due a break anyhow," he says.

SIXTEEN

Instead of a taxi, Jakub insists on taking his car: a four-door Cadillac sedan in a suitably stormy color he claims is called Thunder Gray. Interestingly, it's also the color of his eyes.

After sliding into the roomy passenger seat, I ask Jakub if he minds that I give my editor a call to check in.

"You worried I have a pair of concrete shoes in the trunk?" he asks with a straight face.

"What? No! If I thought you were planning to kill me, I'd have taken you out behind the deli." I snap my fingers. "Like that."

An amused chuckle rumbles in his throat. "Good to know."

Sinking into the plush seat, I place the call.

"You planning to grace us with your presence anytime today?" Stoogan asks the moment he knows it's me. "The publisher wanted to congratulate you on the story this morning, but now he thinks you're snubbing him."

"I'm working," I grumble. "The leads I'm following don't tend to answer the phone."

Stoogan sighs. "Yeah, I know, but try telling that to an accountant. If you're not behind a desk, he thinks you're slacking off."

"Good grief. I don't know how you keep smiling."

"When was the last time you saw me do that?"

"Good point." I change topics. "Have the cops issued any statements today?"

"One. Homeland Security is officially taking over the bombing investigation, but we knew that was coming. John was at the press briefing and managed to ask about your dead bodies on the dock."

"And?"

"Official statement is 'no known connection at this time'. So it's staying in the hands of our local PD."

"Good. PD talks to me, but Homeland Security is so close-lipped half their agents don't know where the toilet is. That's why they always look so uptight."

Stoogan chuckles. "Keep me in the loop."

"Will do."

When I hang up, I check my surroundings and note that the paint has drained from the car to color the day. The few people milling on the streets look void of life and direction, as though we've entered the set piece of a George A. Romero zombie movie.

"Not the best neighborhood to park an expensive car," I say.

Jakub barely blinks. "People here know not to mess with things they shouldn't."

Looking out the window at the pawn shops, liquor stores, and cash advance stores, I say, "Funny, I would have thought the opposite."

"A nice car in a nice neighborhood could belong to anyone," explains Jakub, "a fat housewife, a depressed banker—nameless, faceless, call the cops when they finally notice suspicious people. But a nice car in a bad neighborhood …"

"Could mean the owner is someone you don't want to mess with," I finish.

"Exactly." He flashes an ugly grin. "I don't call the police, but you might wish I had."

Jakub pulls over and parks in the shadow of a six-story brick building that has all the personality of an upended shoe box that's been left out in the rain.

"I feel depressed just looking at it," I say.

Jakub shrugs. "Who are we to judge? Most Americans are one lost paycheck away from the gutter. Everything else is merely an illusion we spin to make ourselves feel better."

"Look at you," I quip as I climb out of the car. "Philosophy major in the making."

"Not in the making," Jakub says as he joins me on the sidewalk. "I earned my master's."

I stare up at him in shock. "Seriously?"

"*Tak*. Why not?"

I try to think of the politest way to put it. "You don't look the type."

Jakub's upper lip curls. "Looks can be deceiving. I thought you were just skinny girl until I talk with my *ciotka* and learn otherwise."

Before we can continue the discussion, Mr. French scuttles out from behind the remains of a long-neglected bus shelter and makes his way over. Jakub eyes his extremely short stature suspiciously until I explain that he's a friend.

When he reaches us, Mr. French looks up at Jakub and gulps. "He's a large fellow."

"And you, not so much," responds Jakub.

Mr. French's perpetual smile wavers. "Quite."

"Gerek still inside?" I ask.

"Yes. Third floor, front apartment on the right."

I look up at the building to see the apartment. There is no discernible movement or flicker of curtains, but a dim light flickers in a variety of red, green, and blue hues from behind the farthest window. I wonder what his preference for afternoon TV is: Judge Judy or the white trash confessional types? I'm betting the latter, despite the tragic consequences it will mean for his language skills.

Mr. French points behind me to the rooftop of a facing building. "Clifford was able to observe the target climb the stairs and enter his apartment. Nobody else appeared present inside, nor has anyone joined him since."

I follow the direction of Mr. French's finger until I spot Clifford sitting on the roof with a high-powered birding scope in his hands.

"Excellent work," I say. "Jakub and I will take it from here."

"You don't need us to stick around for backup?" he asks.

Jakub grunts at the suggestion, but my cold glare shuts him down before he can add any other comment.

"I'd prefer to keep you both as my secret weapons," I tell Mr. French. "I may need to call on you for some more spy work and I don't want your cover blown here."

Mr. French beams with delight. "Of course. You can count on us."

"I know I can." I bend to give him a hug. "You and Clifford get home. I'll pop by for tea later."

"Oh that would be delightful," agrees Mr. French. "But be careful, that Gerek fellow is jumpy as all get out."

I glance up at the apartment and nod. "We will."

———

"You have unusual friends," says Jakub as we climb the stairs to the third floor. "That man is a dwarf."

"Mr. French? I hadn't noticed."

"And why do you call him Mr. French?"

"That's his name."

"You don't call me Mr. Krawiec."

"Would you like me to?"

Jakub ponders it for a moment before letting the thought go.

On the third floor, we stop outside Gerek's door. The hollow veneer looks thin enough to blow down with a sneeze. I quietly try the handle. It's locked.

"What are the chances he's armed?" Jakub asks.

I shrug. "Fifty-fifty."

Exhaling noisily through his nose, Jakub steps to one side of the door and raps with his knuckles. I quickly step to the other side.

After a few moments, a voice calls from inside. "Who's there?"

"Collection agency," says Jakub. "You're behind in your payments."

"*Kurwa!*" bellows Gerek. "It only few weeks, don't you ever give guy fucking break?"

"If you open the door, we can discuss it," says Jakub, his tone surprisingly professional and unthreatening.

"*Idź do diabła!*"

"I speak Polish, *dupek*," Jakub snarls, his demeanor changing in a flash. "And if you don't open the door, I'll make you *zjedz mój chuj*."

"*Kurwa!*" screams Gerek. "Eat this."

The apartment door snaps open to the full length of its safety chain and Gerek's hand darts out to display a five-shot revolver. Before I can scream in surprise, Jakub's hand engulfs it and squeezes so tightly that Gerek's hand is pinned and useless.

"*Kurwa!*" Gerek screams again, but there's more pain in it now than straight fury.

Jakub hits the door with his shoulder, breaking the chain as though it's made of limp spaghetti, which sends Gerek flying backwards until his momentum is halted by the anchor still gripping his hand.

With a noisy crunch of tendons, Gerek's shoulder is wrenched out of its socket before snapping back in place as his knees buckle and he drops to the floor.

Still looking as calm as he did when he was smoking cigarettes behind the deli, Jakub enters the apartment with me at his heels. As I close the door behind us, I notice that none of Gerek's neighbors have bothered to open their doors to see what is going on. Guess they're just thankful it's not them we're after.

With his hand still enveloped around Gerek's, Jakub leads the way down the hall to the living room, dragging the mewling, cursing man behind him.

The only time Gerek goes silent is when he finally realizes someone else is following behind. He looks up to see me and, when recognition dawns, the last of the fight drains from him in a flood.

———

Disarmed, Gerek cradles his crushed hand in his lap. His eyes are the size of saucers as Jakub sits uncomfortably close to him on a flea-bitten couch. I've straddled a wooden kitchen chair to face them.

"My hand is swelling," says Gerek, anger bubbling and popping on every word. "I need ice."

"If we bring you ice," says Jakub in an unemotional monotone, "it will be to keep your severed hand fresh while we cut off the other one."

I wouldn't have said it was possible, but Gerek's eyes grow even wider at the threat.

"Who are you working for?" I ask.

Gerek practically spits. "Whoever pays."

"Who paid last night?"

"That was cash job until you show up. Now, I not paid."

"Who hired you?"

"Bah! You met them."

"I want his name."

Gerek hesitates, but then shrugs. "I do not know name. It not matter to me. Just cash for job."

"You're lying," I say.

Gerek's face flushes red as he prepares to spew his anger, but he chokes on it instead as Jakub grabs his swollen hand and snaps his pinkie. A shard of glistening white bone slices out of the skin as the broken digit hangs at a 45-degree angle.

As Gerek screams in pain, I have to swallow the rising bile in my own throat and remind myself that four women are dead because of men just like him. Jakub's face, on the other hand, never changes expression.

"I'll ask again," I say, desperately trying to remain tough despite my own queasiness. "His name?"

"Patryk," squeals Gerek. "Patryk Graboski."

"He was the one in charge last night?"

"*Tak!*"

"And who does he work for?"

"I don't know."

Jakub grabs his hand again and Gerek bursts into tears. "I swear. *Kurwa!* I don't know."

Jakub hesitates, but then breaks the man's index finger anyway.

Gerek howls as tears run from his eyes and snot bubbles in his nose.

"Do you have an address for Patryk?" I ask, staying tough.

"Just phone. He calls when he has job."

"And what is the work?" I ask.

"Transport."

"Of women?"

Gerek flinches as Jakub moves his hand, but it's only to scratch his nose.

Gerek nods rapidly. "We load women in van and take from docks to building. I not go inside. I am paid and I go."

"I'll need that address."

Gerek blurts it out without any further coercion.

"One last question."

Gerek looks relieved.

"Is Red Swan involved?" I ask.

Gerek swallows. "I not know. I-I-I work for Patryk. We not discuss matter of business."

I exchange a look with Jakub, the movement causing a strange burble to rise in Gerek's throat.

"I swear," he blurts. "I am nothing. Transport only, no more. I don't want to know."

After a moment of silence, I produce a folded piece of paper from my pocket and unfold it to show the composite that Frank gave me. "Who is this?"

Gerek glances at the photo and then back up at my face. "I not know him."

"Are you sure? Look closely."

Jakub moves his large hand back down to touch the back of Gerek's swollen one.

Jakub nods his head so rapidly, I worry that he's going to snap it.

"I sure," he gasps. "He not even look Polish."

I replace the paper in my pocket and ask, "Where is your phone?"

His eyes shift toward a small table at the far end of the couch. I stand up and retrieve a pay-as-you-go cell. Scrolling through its menu, I find the incoming calls and Patryk's number.

"Do you have any other phones on the premises?" I ask.

Gerek shakes his head.

"Any other weapons?"

He shakes his head again.

"OK, here's what we're going to do."

———

Outside Gerek's apartment, Jakub asks, "Are you sure about this?"

"You should go," I answer as we descend the stairs. "I'll be fine and Eddie will be wondering where the heck you've disappeared to."

"You don't know what that *dupek* will say. He could get us both in trouble."

"He's far too macho to admit he was beat up by a girl, and you were never here."

"Perhaps, but lawyers will use any trick even for scum like him."

"Go," I insist as we reach street level. "I've got this."

As Jakub reluctantly returns to his Cadillac, I pull out my phone and call Frank.

"You busy?" I ask when he answers.

"Always. Why?"

"I've tracked down one of the men involved in the death of those four women last night. He's holed up in his apartment right now and I'm willing to bet he knows who else is involved."

The phone is muffled for a moment as Frank covers the receiver to purge a mouthful of profanity. I could be wrong, but I'm sure it's not directed at me.

When he comes back on the line, a stern concern coats his words. "And where are you?"

"Across the street. Making sure he stays put."

"Stay there," he orders. "Don't go any closer."

"Wouldn't dream of it."

———

When the SWAT team drags Gerek out of the building and dumps him into the back of a patrol car, I film it on my phone. If Gerek sees me, he doesn't let on, but judging by the terrified, defeated look on his face, I'd be surprised if he even noticed.

When Frank returns, I take him off to the side and hand him Gerek's phone.

"He dropped this," I say. "And there's a contact on it that you need to see."

Frank sighs heavily as he takes the phone. "He dropped it?"

"Before he did, however," I continue, ignoring his incredulity. "I heard him mention the address of where he was taking the women."

"Convenient."

I ignore the sarcasm too. "If you raid it now before word of his arrest gets out, there's a good chance you may be able to save some people."

"I would need a warrant."

"Easy," I insist. "What judge wouldn't want to be a hero on this? Women are being held against their will and turned into sex slaves. You could shut this down and save some of them."

Frank grits his teeth. "I don't operate on a whim, Dixie. There's rules."

"Fuck the rules! We're talking about lives."

Frank's eyes harden into black stones for a moment before softening again. He glances over at Gerek, sitting handcuffed and alone in the back seat of the patrol car.

"He'll confirm this?"

I nod. "Ask him directly. He doesn't appear to have much fight left in him."

"Wonder why that is."

I shrug. "Tough neighborhood?"

Frank turns his back to me and heads for the patrol car.

SEVENTEEN

FRANK ALLOWS ME TO ride along, but once we arrive at the address provided by Gerek, I'm left a safe and boring distance away while SWAT storms the building.

Catching its occupants by surprise, the raid is over faster than I would have thought possible. The heavily armed tactical team takes each floor with choreographed precision, and despite a propensity for smoke grenades and disorienting flash-bangs, the only real trouble is several short bursts of automatic gunfire on the third floor.

When Frank—looking like a badass in his Kevlar vest and AR-15 assault rifle—emerges from the building, he is trailed by at least a dozen terrified and bedraggled women. A short time later, Patryk Graboski is dragged out in handcuffs by four burly, armor-clad SWAT officers. Although his face is bloody, he appears to have made it through without much additional damage. Pity.

I don't bother waving.

As Frank bellows orders for more officers, ambulances, and specialists to be brought to the scene, I use my phone to call for a taxi. This simple act makes me wonder how I ever lived without the phone, but I try not to enjoy the feeling.

Dixie's Tips #27: *Becoming dependent on something doesn't mean you can't go back to doing without. It's dealing with the loss that's difficult because you'll always know what you're missing. That's why I've avoided trying the lemon maple Cronut.*

Waiting on the fringe, drooling slightly at the thought of a lemon maple Cronut, I'm surprised when Frank breaks away from the uniformed pack and walks over.

"Good work, Detective Sergeant Fury," I say in my best imitation of a television news broadcaster. "It appears you've broken a sex slavery ring connected with the recent suspicious deaths of four women at the dockyards. What's next? Are you going to Disneyland?"

Frank doesn't crack a smile. "There's going to be a lot of that, isn't there?"

"Yup. I can hear the media scrambling to get their cameras down here now. Helicopters will be circling overhead any minute, probably just taking an extra second to let the young reporters touch up the bronzer on their cleavage. I would suggest calling the brass and the mayor, they'll definitely want their pound of coverage. Just make sure they publicly pat you on the back and don't take all the glory for themselves."

Frank cringes. "It was a solid tip, Dix. And even though I don't want to know how you came by it, these women have a lot to thank you for."

"Maybe," I say, turning serious. "Who knows what kind of life they left behind, but I sure as hell don't believe this is what they expected to find when they got here. Any trouble inside? I heard gunfire."

Frank shrugs dismissively. "We ran into some resistance on the third floor. Two wounded. One dead. Paramedics are with the injured now."

"All bad guys?"

Frank nods.

"Any sign of our bomb guy?" I ask, knowing the odds are slim.

"That's still off the record, but I scrutinized every face and he's not inside."

Sirens fill the air as more ambulances arrive to transport the women to the hospital. Frank tells me most of them are dehydrated, starved, and in desperate need of a long bath. Unlike what Hollywood may try to portray, most sex slaves are raped and abused rather then pampered and seduced.

"If any of them feel like talking, I'd like to write their stories," I say. "Might help with public perception. People hear *sex slave* and the only word they can relate is *whore*. They don't imagine the path it took to get these women here."

"I'll pass the word."

A horn beeps and I turn to see my taxi waiting.

"Dog House later?" I ask.

Frank looks over his shoulder at the chaos. "If I can get away."

"Delegate," I say. "You're the hero. You deserve a beer—even if it is only O'Doul's."

Frank trumps my smirk with a crinkled grin. "See you around eight."

"Oh, and one more thing," I add as I back away. "Keep the Kevlar vest on for the cameras. It looks *hot*."

I turn before I can witness Frank's reaction, preferring to think he's smiling rather than giving me the finger.

———

"You just missed John," Stoogan bellows across the newsroom when I appear. "Did you hear about the raid? John's on his way down there. You can still—"

I tap the side of my head with my index finger. "Already been, just need to write it up."

"Seriously?" Stoogan looks perplexed. "The scanners have only—"

I hold my phone aloft. "Even have video of it in progress, although I'm not sure how to get it off the phone."

"Gillian!" Stoogan bellows even louder. "Get that video on the web, now!"

A tiny young blonde with the moon-eyed face of a cartoon pixie—and the fashion sense to match—rushes over to snatch my phone.

"Just don't look at the private ones," I warn before letting go. "Mary Jane's been doing a piece on sexting, and she borrowed my phone to do some salacious stuff. With those peepers, it could seriously blind you."

When the young reporter fails to smile, I'm forced to admit, "It's a joke."

She still doesn't smile.

"Like I would seriously give my phone to Mary Jane to take photos of her hoo-ha," I add incredulously.

The reporter continues to stare at me like I've grown an extra head before she finds her momentum again and vanishes into the maze of desks, my phone clutched in her hand like a prized coin in an arcade game.

"Is it me?" I say aloud, but nobody answers.

———

After filing my story, Stoogan and I discuss a few legal logistics about what I can and can't include before he clicks the button to make the whole thing active on our website.

In the meantime, Gillian has downloaded all the video off my phone and expertly edited it down into manageable chunks. She knits the video into the story and, with Stoogan's approval, makes it live on the web, too.

It all feels so … underwhelming.

"I think you should get a pail of printer's ink and set it in the corner of your office," I tell Stoogan. "Then when you have a breaking story, you can pry off the lid and let everyone take a big whiff. Clicking a mouse just doesn't have the same …" I struggle for the word, but only the French seem to have what I'm searching for: "*Je ne sais quoi.*"

Stoogan chuckles. "Yeah, and maybe I'll hire a retired pressman to stand behind me and yell all the reasons why there's 'no fucking way I'm stopping the fucking press, I don't care how fucking big the fucking story is'."

We both burst out laughing while Gillian, who has arrived in the doorway to return my phone, stares at us as if we've both lost our senses.

"You need something?" Stoogan asks the young reporter as he wipes his eyes.

"Err, I-I just wanted to let you know that the hits are going crazy on this already. We're the first ones up with a full story and it's trending on Twitter."

Stoogan looks across his desk at me and winks. "Guess we're not too old for this game after all."

I glance up at the clock. "Beer?"

"Thought you'd never ask."

EIGHTEEN

AFTER DRINKS WITH THE boss, I'm welcomed home by a knowing wink from King William, who is sitting regally in Mrs. Pennell's front window. When I reach up to touch the glass, he bumps it with his forehead to acknowledge our kinship.

In the lobby, I check the mail. After discarding the pizza flyers and No Credit Check Loan Guaranteed junk, I'm left with a tiny package wrapped in blood-colored paper. The box is so small that there is barely enough room on its surface for a stamp and address.

Like the other mysterious parcels, the handwriting isn't particularly neat or enlightening. However, it's still legible enough to maneuver its way through the postal system without rejection.

A door opens and Mr. French appears.

I hold up the package between my fingers to show him.

"What number is this?" he asks.

"Four."

"Would you like to open it inside? I have the kettle on."

When I hesitate, he adds, "I also have a lovely French brandy that I've been wanting to uncork, but I do so hate to drink alone."

Baccarat chirps her delight when I enter the apartment and settle on the love seat. Mr. French cracks the wax seal on the brandy and pours a generous amount of honey-amber liquid into two crystal snifters. After handing me one of the bowl-shaped glasses, he buries his nose into the rim of his and inhales so deeply his toes practically lift off the ground.

"My, my," he says. "I dare say Napoleon himself would be impressed."

I take a tentative sniff of my own drink before plunging ahead with a sip. The brandy is full of complex citrus notes that swirl as much in my head as they do on my tongue. The heat it releases as it slides down my throat is both soothing and intense.

Mr. French reads my face and smiles. "Not too shabby?"

"Dare I ask how much that bottle cost?"

Mr. French waves away the question. "Let's not spoil it with talk of money."

After the third sip, every muscle softens and I feel the force of gravity pulling on individual bones as though my whole skeleton is being loosened from the inside out. Before I turn into a lazy octopus, I lay the small package on the coffee table and carefully unwrap it.

Inside is a tile matching the previous three in shape and color. It is also the second one with the letter I painted on its face. The bonus prize is a small brass hook with a slightly elongated neck that ends in a T-shaped crossbar.

"What's the hook for?" asks Mr. French.

"To complete the gallows. All I'm missing now is the rope."

"And the body," says Mr. French.

I look over at him. "That's the part that's worrying me."

"Ah, quite." Mr. French takes another sip of brandy. "I'm afraid I couldn't come up with many answers on the paper. Its color is certainly vivid, but not unique. Except . . ." He hesitates.

"Go on," I press.

"Clifford says it's not gift wrap. The paper is too thick and it has a waxy coating on the inside, which means it's for commercial use."

"What type of commerce?"

"Butchery. The wax coating prevents blood from soaking into the paper."

"Great." I take a large swallow of brandy and the heat of it rises within me. "So it's not a secret admirer with a twisted sense of romance? It's a goddamn butcher."

"Not necessarily," says Mr. French. "Those supplies are available to anyone who carves meat: hunters, fishermen—"

"So not necessarily a licensed butcher," I interrupt, words sliding around my mouth without constraint. "Just someone who enjoys cutting up dead things."

"Quite." Mr. French pales. "Sorry. Should I have kept it to myself?"

I finish my drink and close my eyes for a second to restore balance. "No," I say finally. "It's best that I know everything, but I need a favor."

"Anything."

"Can we keep this between ourselves? I don't want Mrs. Pennell to worry that I'm bringing more danger to her doorstep. She still hasn't recovered from the last incident."

"My lips are sealed, but *are* you in danger?"

I shrug off the question. "Who knows? This could easily be a practical joke. Somebody wanting to frighten me for something that I've written."

"The woman with the bomb?"

I shake my head. "The first package arrived before I met her. I don't see a connection."

Mr. French retrieves the brandy bottle, but I turn down his offer of a refill and make my excuses to leave.

"Before you go," says Mr. French, "can I ask about your story that's on the web now? I noticed the man you had me follow is mentioned very briefly at the end. He doesn't appear to be of much significance."

"He's not," I say, "at least not any more. But there was no story without him. Gerek was a thread that needed pulling, and when we did—thanks to you and Clifford—the story broke wide open." I move forward and wrap the diminutive man in a hug. "You helped break up a slave ring today."

When I release him, Mr. French is grinning from ear to ear. "That's rather impressive," he says proudly.

"It is," I agree, finding my smile again. "And we definitely deserved that brandy."

We both laugh as Mr. French escorts me to the door.

———

In my apartment, I place the fourth tile on its stand. The letters now spell DIXI_ with one space left to fill. The metal hook, its glistening bend awaiting a rope, snaps perfectly into a groove on the tip of the inverted-L's horizontal arm.

Stepping back, I have to admire the skill that went into making the macabre miniature. But for the life of me, I have no idea who has sent it or why.

Prince Marmalade jumps onto my lap the moment I—still fully dressed in my street clothes, having not had the will to even take off my boots—collapse onto the couch. Before he can settle, however, his nose twitches and he moves to explore the pocket of my coat.

Remembering what's inside, I pull out the smoked meat sandwich Mario made for me earlier in the day. My stomach gurgles at the beefy aroma as I unwrap the translucent waxed paper. The sandwich has been crushed in my neglect, but it still looks perfectly edible.

"Want to share?" I ask Prince, but the question is moot as he's already starting to drool.

Tearing off a chunk of meat, I allow Prince to eat it on my lap while I munch down on the rest. When we're done, I scrunch the greasy paper into a ball and toss it onto the coffee table. Prince races after it as I slump to one side and close my eyes for a few minutes of rest.

The respite doesn't last, as Prince hisses in fear in the same moment that something soft and rubbery bumps my nose. When I open my eyes, a large yellow balloon with a smiley face drawn on its surface is floating inches from my face.

"What the hell?"

Snatching the balloon out of the air, I read the small card attached to its tail. It's identical to the one I threw in the trash this morning: the single word *Hello,* but with the *o* replaced with a circle of solid red.

Turning to Prince, I ask, "Have you been throwing parties while I'm at work?"

Prince tilts his head slightly, but the arch in his back tells me he's as confused about the balloon as I am.

With balloon in hand, I march across the hall to Kristy and Sam's apartment, where I knock and wait. When Sam opens the door, her face is red and puffy, but the ear-to-ear grin tells me it's not from watching Jane Austen movies.

"Dixie!" she squeals and wraps me in an unusually warm embrace. "When did you get home?"

"Just now. What's going on. Have you been crying?"

Sam grabs my arm and drags me into the apartment where Kristy's face is just as tear-stained and happy as her partner's. The lightbulb flicks on, but I keep it hidden under a crinkled brow as Sam rushes to Kristy's side and pulls her to her feet.

"We want you to be the first to know," says Sam excitedly, squeezing Kristy's hand.

I prepare myself and hope that my face is a total blank. "Tell me what?"

"We're pregnant!"

My jaw drops to emphasize my look of surprise as I rush forward to embrace both women. Together, the three of us dance, hug, cry, and laugh in celebration over a tiny, barely detectable life.

All thoughts of the balloon are forgotten as it slips from my hand and floats away.

———

I'm startled awake when my cellphone comes alive on the nightstand. For such a small device, it packs a lighthouse full of glaring brightness and foghorn noise that makes me completely forget **Dixie's Tips #1:** *When a phone rings in the middle of the night, it's never good news.*

"Hello?" I burble into the receiver after struggling to glide my finger across the right button. My bedroom is pitch black, which tells me whatever the hell time it is, it's too goddamn early.

"Dixie?" whispers a timid voice.

"Half of her," I snap. "The other half is still sleeping. Who is this?"

"It's Berta."

"Berta? What are you doing? It must be the middle of the night."

"I saw him."

"Who?"

"The man in the picture."

"The picture?" I struggle to wake up, realizing the young woman is talking about Frank's photo composite. "The bomber? Are you sure?"

"He has large mark on cheek and steel in his ear. It's him."

"Where are you?"

"On street. I was in club. They don't check ID, so I can do drinking. He was in VIP section."

"Are you still there?"

"He leave club, so I follow."

"Don't!" I blurt. "He's dangerous."

"He not see me."

"Have you called Irena or Matylda?"

"No. They not like me visit club, but I am young, not dead. And in the dark, boys find me pretty."

As my consciousness rises into full alert mode, I hear the cheerful lubrication in her voice, the false bravado unlocked through inebriation.

"Tell me where you are and I'll meet you."

"I—" She hesitates and lowers her voice even further. "He is here again. I thought he gone inside for night, but he come back out."

"Does he see you?"

"No, no, looking other way. He moving again. I follow."

"Tell me where you are," I demand, my tone turning harsh.

"I do not want to lose him."

"Tell me where you are," I repeat. "We'll go together."

The phone crackles and I fear I've lost her, but then she comes back on the line and whispers an address.

"I follow," she repeats before the line goes dead.

NINETEEN

Stepping out of the cab, I'm dressed for trouble with Lily the knife in my boot and a lead-filled sap—a present from Pinch—in the pocket of my green coat. After an internal debate about the legality of concealed carry when you don't possess the appropriate permit, I chose to leave the Governor at home. I only hope I don't regret the decision.

If New York is the city that never sleeps, San Francisco is where things scurry around in the dark. With the tourists tucked up in their hotel beds for the night, most panhandlers return to their makeshift shelters in doorways, alleys, and the inner-city parks least likely to be patrolled by cops and cruel opportunists.

In those wee hours between the late-night partiers running out of steam and the early-risers of commerce and trade starting their day, every moving shadow is a question mark: Friend or foe? Human or animal? Lost or found?

After giving my eyes a short time to adjust, I scour the empty streets but see no sign of Berta.

I move to stand beneath a halogen streetlamp, its yellow light falling in a sputter like rain, and slowly rotate 360 degrees in the hope she'll make her presence known.

"Yeh ain't gonna find no trade this time o' night, Red," a voice cackles from a nearby doorway. "All dem johns gone home to wifey."

Focusing in on the spot, I spy an elderly woman beneath a tattered indigo blanket. Apart from tufts of wiry gray hair frozen above dull, jaundiced eyes, her face is a blank slate that blends with the night as though cut from the same sheet of tar paper.

"I'm looking for a friend," I say. "Young woman, slender, about my height." I touch the side of my face. "She has burns."

The woman nods. "I seen 'er."

"Do you know where she went?"

"She was followin' that cruel bastard who live roun' here. Ya move yer eyes when he's passin' cause he's as likely to spit in yer face or kick ya in the ribs fer bein' in his line of sight. Prick."

My stomach sours. "That's what I'm worried about. Which way did she go?"

The woman pokes a knuckled finger out from beneath the blanket to point down the street. Then, just as quickly, she points in the opposite direction. "He live back thatta way, but"—her finger flips 180 degrees back to the first position—"he spend most time down there somewhere. He ain't right."

"You don't know where he goes?" I press.

"Not my concern. He trouble, plain an' true, but he ain't givin' alms to the poor, that's fer damn sure."

I dig in my pocket to find some change and come up with a few small bills. "Thanks," I say as I hand them over.

"Ain't no thing," says the woman, "but I thank yeh fer buyin' breakfast."

I take off down the street, glancing into every nook and cranny, hoping to find Berta huddled in a doorway somewhere and regretting her decision to play spy in the nighttime while wearing flimsy club gear. But most of all, I just want her to be safe.

At the end of the block, I stop to survey the four-way intersection. The block directly ahead of me is cluttered with dark storefronts, heavy bars and shutters pulled down over their display windows and doors. To my left, modern condo towers climb toward the sky in an effort to provide some kind of view or just escape the noise and pollution of busy streets.

I decide to turn right, where the buildings are still made of soot-covered brick, the windows boxy and small, and the sidewalks narrow. Halfway down, I spy the glow of a smartphone escaping the dank doorway of a shuttered second-hand store with a large For Lease sign in its empty window.

"Berta?" I call out.

The light goes dim as thick fingers try to cover its screen.

I rush toward the doorway. "Berta?"

The grimy face that looks up from amidst a disorganized pile of mismatched, oversized clothes reminds me of a doll I saw once at a craft fair with strands of wool for hair and a head made from a shrunken, dried apple. If every wrinkle tells a story, this man is wearing a library on his leathered face.

The phone in his grubby hands is bright pink with a childish decal of an overly cute, unicorn-pony hybrid on its rear panel.

"Where did you get that phone?" I ask.

The man stares at me through cloudy, cataract eyes and rolls a gray tongue across dry, cracked lips. "It's mine," he growls.

"Cut the crap," I snarl. "Where did you get it?"

"What do you care?"

Biting my tongue, I dig into the front pocket of my jeans and pull out a crumpled ten-dollar bill whose last adventure was to bankroll a bet on a dog race.

"I'll buy it from you if you tell me where you got it."

The man's eyes widen in covetous curiosity. "Worth more than ten bucks."

"How about ten bucks and I don't kick you in the nuts?"

The man licks his lips again and holds out his free hand for the money. I keep a tight hold of one end of the bill until he hands over the phone, then we let go of both items in unison.

The phone's screen is badly cracked, but it's still working. I check the number. It's Berta's.

"Where did you get it?" I press.

The man shrugs. "Found it."

"Where?"

He points across the street at a boarded-up, six-story brick building that's surely designated to be gutted and turned into another condo tower once the developer comes up with enough cash. Like most cities around the country, real estate speculators left carcasses in their wake when their wallets got burned by the sudden economic downturn. Although on the mend, many are still licking their wounds.

"Did you see who dropped it?" I ask.

The man's eyes shift away as he prepares to lie.

"Don't!" I snap. "Just tell me the goddamn truth."

He lowers his chin to his chest. "Girl dropped it when a man grabbed her."

"Shit!" Panic rises in my chest and I have to talk myself into remaining calm. "This man—blonde, sharp nose, birthmark on his cheek?"

The man shrugs. "Could be. My eyes ain't worth shit no more."

I look back at the building, calculating. "How many people inside?"

"Fuck knows. They come and go all hours."

"Ballpark?"

"No idea. Two, ten—what am I, a calculator?"

I flash him my teeth, and not in a friendly way, before slipping Berta's phone into my pocket.

"How do I get inside?"

The man exposes his own teeth, or at least what's left of them. "Wood on the door is for show. It looks locked, but ain't nobody ever use a key."

———

After a quick eyeball of the area to make sure there are no unexpected surprises, I flatten my body against the wall and reach out tentatively for the door. Planks of knotty wood have been nailed across its surface and a large, plastic yellow sign is bolted in place to warn potential squatters the building is condemned and trespassers will be prosecuted. But, as Prune Face pointed out, it's mostly for show.

Somebody has taken a thin saw to the planks, freeing the seam around the doorway so it still operates as intended. The industrial hinges are stiff, the door used to being yanked rather than eased. My fingers ache as I slowly, one quarter-inch at a time, pull the door open enough that I can get an eyeball to the crack and a limited view inside.

A lone lightbulb in an adjoining room spills murky light into the entryway through its own cracked door, allowing me to see an old, iron-gated elevator to my left, a haphazard barrier of broken furniture and scrap wood blocking the long hallway that leads to the rear of the building, and a wide set of stained concrete steps leading to the deeper abyss of the upper levels.

The room directly to my right is where the lightbulb hangs. Its door is cracked open, but only by a few inches. Not being able to trust my eyes, I focus on my hearing. A radio, its volume turned low, is playing in the room, but the reception is bad and the hiss is more static than music.

I pull the leather sap out of my pocket, its leaded weight reassuring in my hand, and ease the street door as far as I dare. I don't need much to slip inside, but every inch wider causes another spark of anxiety.

Somebody coughs inside the lit room and a wooden chair creaks with the weight of a fidgeting body. Holding my breath, I finally leave the street and slip into the dark hollow of the building's lobby.

Remembering to breathe again, I carefully release my weight from the door and allow it to glide back into place. Obediently, it eases closed, but instead of resting on the jamb, its weight forces it to shut completely and the click of the latch sounds more like a thunderclap.

Shit! I freeze in place, my lungs shriveling inside my chest as my mind goes into panicked overdrive.

Stop it! I yell inside my head, fighting to remember my lessons with Pinch. *You are in control. Use the adrenaline, don't let it use you.* Or as Yoda would say: *A pussy don't be.*

Dixie's Tips #28: *Experts will tell you that the opposite of being scared is confidence, but confidence can crack. I've always found that humor is the best antidote. Laughter turns any purchase that fear can grab onto into greasy green goose poop.*

The clink of the latch doesn't register with whoever is inside the lit room, which gives me time to settle my nerves and balance my stance.

I lean forward to peer through the crack in the door when a woman's scream pierces the air above me. It's instantly followed by a string of Polish curses and, sickeningly, the knuckles-on-meat sound of a fist striking soft flesh.

Before I can react, the door I'm facing is yanked open and a large man in a sweat-stained T-shirt fills the doorway. Behind him on the floor is a set of plastic dumbbells, but it's the large weapon in his hands, rather than his engorged biceps, that gives me pause.

Fortunately, he's more surprised to find me blocking his way than I am to see him.

The sap rises of its own accord as my body automatically changes position to bring my full weight down on top of it. The lead-filled pouch cracks his skull slightly above his left ear, sending the other side of his head crashing into the sharp edge of the door jamb. His eyes roll white in his crushed head as I snatch the shotgun out of his limp hands before his knees buckle and he drops.

Stunned by the effectiveness of my own brutality, I bend down to touch the man's thick neck. He's still breathing, but completely out cold. I'll need to remember to send Pinch a box of chocolates along with a thank-you note.

Apart from the unconscious body, the rest of the room is unoccupied.

Dropping the sap back into my pocket, I make sure the shotgun is loaded and return to the stairs.

Sweating profusely, I creep up with the barrel of the gun pointing the way.

———

On the first landing, the hallway seems to stretch for miles with closed doors on either side. At the far end, where the window to the fire escape should be, a large sheet of plywood blocks most of the outside light.

The only interior light spills from beneath the doors of four rooms, which makes me wish I had brought a flashlight or, even better, night-vision goggles. I'm sure Pinch owns a pair.

Moving to the closest room, I press my ear to the door and listen. Somebody inside is snoring, but the television is still on. Either a second person is watching the Shopping Channel or sleepyhead reached his endurance limit and decided to take a rest.

I move to the next door. This time I hear a woman weeping and the sound of heavy footsteps pacing back and forth across the floor. I count the footsteps, weighing the sound level against the distance traveled. Twelve steps in one direction, turn, twelve steps back, turn.

Taking a deep breath, I balance the shotgun in my right hand and place my left on the door handle. When I figure the pacer is roughly ten steps away from the door and with his back to me, I turn the handle and step into the room.

Slumped on the floor with blood dripping from her nose and mouth, Berta gasps when she sees me enter with the pump-action shotgun gripped menacingly in my hands.

The blonde man at the other end of the room, however, turns and offers a cold smile as though expecting me.

"You're her gang?" he asks, the hint of an English accent in his voice, ignoring the gun leveled at his chest. "Your friend warned me she belongs to a gang of ruthless women, but"—he raises his arms to show he isn't armed—"this is disappointing."

"Stay where you are," I warn before turning to Berta. "Are you OK?"

Berta spits blood on the floor. "I've had worse. He hits like little girl."

The blonde sniggers. "Feisty. Gotta love it."

"You make one move and I'll show you fucking feisty."

The blonde's smile fades to a thin line and he squares his shoulders in challenge. "I'd like to see that."

"Come on," I say to Berta. "We're getting out of here."

"An optimist," says the blonde. "Those are a rare commodity. Last optimist I knew blew his brains out in a game of Russian roulette. Course, I was holding the gun at the time."

"If you try to stop us—"

"Wouldn't dream of it," interrupts the blonde. "But you don't really believe I'm alone, do you?"

I stare into clear, cerulean eyes and find a dark hollow where a soul should be. And despite every nerve ending and instinct telling me to grab Berta and run like hell, I have to ask: "Did you plant a bomb inside Ania?"

The blonde tilts his head to one side and the line of his lips slithers into a concerned ripple. "Who are you?"

I ignore his question. "Did you?"

His eyes flick to Berta and then back to me. "Is that why she was following me? You knew Ania?"

"Did you kill her?" I snap.

"She killed herself. Everyone saw that. It was even on the news."

"Because of you and what you did to her."

He tilts his head to the other side like a hyena plotting the best way to rip out an enemy's throat, but I can tell he's genuinely troubled.

"How did you piece that together?"

"Just answer the question," I demand, baring my teeth. "Did you plant a bomb in her womb?"

His cold smile returns and the large birthmark on his cheek grows darker. "I did. With a little help from some friends, of course. But . . ." He stops talking.

"But?" I press.

The smile evaporates to reveal his true self as though even that false mask takes concentrated effort. "But I don't like you knowing that."

"Well, too fuc—"

He snaps his fingers and the loud, frantic scramble of thick claws on bare wood makes me spin to the far side of the room where two coal-black Doberman Pinschers charge from dark corners. Their enlarged chest muscles ripple and their sharp teeth are shiny with saliva.

The highly-trained animals hadn't made a singular sound the entire time I was in the room—and they move faster than I can.

I yank the trigger to fire blindly in their direction, hoping the noise will buy me time, but the heavily muscled dogs barely blink as the lethal slugs soar over their heads to tear fist-sized chunks out of the far wall. Before I can reload, the dogs are on me. I scream as one sinks its teeth into my arm while the other chomps down on my left leg and shakes its head to knock me off balance.

As I fall to the floor, I lash out with the rifle butt and smash the dog's skull. The animal still doesn't make a sound as it momentarily releases its grip on my leg before shaking off the blow and biting down once more.

On the ground, I'm at their mercy, and my only thought is to curl into a ball, protecting my face, neck, and internal organs from their teeth. Berta shrieks at the dogs and begs the blonde man to call off the attack, but her frantic pleas fall on deaf ears.

The dogs claw and rip at my green coat, desperately trying to flip me over so they can sink their maws into my stomach and burrow deep inside for the sweet meat and pungent offal. I try to reach my knife, but every attempt is blocked as the dogs nip at my hand with enough force to remove a finger in a single bite.

The door opens behind me and a bulky shadow grunts with pleasure at the sight of my attack.

"End it," says the blonde, his voice calm, almost bored.

I curl into a tighter ball in a final act of defiance, preferring a bullet to being ripped apart by savage teeth.

An unexpected blow to the base of my skull sends a fireball of pain shooting through every inch of my body, causing my muscles to unclench. The last thing I hear is the dogs chuffing in triumph before a second blow turns everything black.

TWENTY

PAIN. IT FILLS MY body as I struggle to rise from the darkness, my consciousness pulling itself hand over hand up a slippery rope before forcing open the gauzy covering of thin flesh that blinds my sight.

With a groan, my eyelids flutter and my head spins. I try to move, to stretch cramped muscles, but another wave of pain makes my stomach lurch.

A plastic bowl is thrust into my hands as someone places a hand on my chest and another on my back to hold me steady while I purge.

"You're back," says Berta. "You have me very worry."

Wiping my lips on the back of my hand, I need Berta's help to sit up and lean against a water-damaged lathe-and-plaster wall. It takes another moment for my head to stop spinning and fall into a rhythm of throbbing pain. Reaching back to the base of my skull, my hand returns with traces of blood.

My left leg, its denim covering sliced away above the knee, is bandaged with makeshift strips of torn clothing. My right leg and arm appear mostly unscathed, but another makeshift bandage covers my left forearm. There's no sign of my lucky coat.

"We clean wounds best we can," explains Berta, "but not lot here to use. No antiseptic, no alcohol, no medicine, just water and soap. We bandage two worst."

"Who's *we*?" I ask, moving my jaw from side to side to check for loose teeth.

Berta moves to one side, exposing the dingy room beyond. A huddle of young women peer back at me, their faces as gaunt and afraid as their bellies are swollen.

"Are they pregnant or—"

"Pregnant," says Berta. "They let me feel babies kick."

"How many?"

"Six, plus you and me."

"The men?"

Berta shrugs. "They lock door and leave."

I indicate the women. "How long have they been here?"

Berta speaks to the women in Polish. "They come by boat and brought here many months ago. None were pregnant at time."

"They were raped?" I ask.

Berta speaks to the women again in their native tongue. When she turns back to me, her face is ash.

"Many times." Her mouth is dry. "They are rented for sex without condoms. When they get pregnant, they moved here. And there are more in other rooms."

"All pregnant?"

"Some yes, some no."

"Where are the babies?" I ask, recalling Ania's cesarian scar.

Berta asks the women, but none of them seem to know.

"Jesus!" I attempt to get to my feet, but nausea drags me back down. Cursing again, I reach into my back pocket for my phone only to discover that, as to be expected, it's gone.

"Is my coat around?" I ask.

"They take it from you before throwing us here." She crinkles her nose. "It was horrible mess. Dogs fight over it."

With a groan, I reach out to grab her shoulder. "Help me to my feet."

Berta studies me through concerned eyes. "You need rest to recover."

"No, we need to get the hell out of here." I glance across at the pregnant women. "All of us."

Every inch of my ascent from ass to feet is agony. My back, ribs, legs, and arms are a mess of bruises, bites, rips, and tears. Every part of me screams to stop moving, but I'm nothing if not stubborn.

Finally, I stand erect, but the exertion has peppered my face with perspiration and left me fighting for breath. I gulp shallow lungfuls of air; the bruising from the dogs' vicious attack has seeped deep into my chest, making even the expansion of my ribs painful.

I feel the eyes of the other women upon me and know that I need to grit my teeth and fight to be strong if we're ever going to stand a chance of escape.

Before I can display a brave face, however, a heavy bolt thunders back and the door opens. The blonde enters with two muscled henchmen by his side. One of the henchmen is the guard from downstairs who I knocked unconscious with my sap. He's staring at me like I'm a marbled steak—cooked rare with crispy fried onions and just a sprinkling of coarse sea salt.

The blonde has the remains of my coat in one hand and a folded piece of paper in the other.

"I'm surprised you're on your feet," he says, dropping my coat to the floor and kicking it to one side. "Must be that plank-thick Irish skull."

"I'm not one to sit around and twiddle my thumbs," I reply, trying to sound tougher than I feel.

The smile falters. "You like my dogs? Misch and Hentschel."

"I'm more of a cat person."

One of the henchmen snickers but catches himself before his boss has time to turn his head and flash a warning.

"Oh, but they liked you," says the blonde, "and can't wait for another chance to play."

I have a witty comeback about smothering his balls in peanut butter as an appetizer, but I keep it to myself.

His cold smile returns. "I have been reading all about you, Dixie Flynn of *NOW* magazine."

"If you know my name, then you know people will be missing me."

The smile flickers and his nose wrinkles. "But not enough to text or call. Your phone hasn't made a Little Bo Peep."

This time I don't have a comeback. It takes all my energy just to stand straight and not display the weakness that pulsates through every fiber of my battered body.

The blonde unwraps the sheet of paper, exposing Frank's photo composite. It had been in the pocket of my coat, along with the sap and Berta's phone.

"Where did you get this?" he asks.

I debate whether it's smarter to lie or tell the truth, but in that split-second of indecision, one of the henchmen steps forward and I know for certain that I can't withstand any more pain.

"The police," I say, stopping the henchman in his tracks.

"And how did they get it?"

"From video footage at the bombing."

"Ahh." He moves his head from side to side like a cobra sensing its prey. "For decades we worry about the rise of Big Brother only to line up in queues to become exactly that. Forget surveillance cameras; the watchers and the watched are now one in the same. Ironic or what?"

"Why did you do it?" I ask, closing down the banter.

The blonde's eyes narrow. "Why do you think?"

"No idea."

"But you have a theory." There is heat in his voice. "Even now, even here, you can't stop being the nosy bitch."

"I was there," I say, my eyes burning. "Ania asked to talk with me before she jumped. Mine was the last face she saw."

The blonde is taken aback and his eyes widen with surprise. "What did she tell you?"

"That's just it. Nothing. She didn't care about you or whatever your fucked-up plans are. She simply wanted her story told. I thought she was noble, a scared child who didn't want her life to be empty of meaning, but now I see how completely broken she was. She could have told us about you." I wave my arm to encompass the huddle of pregnant women. "And about them. But you had her so brainwashed that she gave me nothing."

"And yet you're here." His face flares in anger and he crumples the paper in his hand before throwing it at me. "How did the filth get my face?"

"You triggered the bomb," I snap back. "If you didn't want the attention, you should have stayed out of the spotlight. Homeland Security is on this now and they have way more resources than SFPD."

With a frustrated hiss, the blonde snaps a trembling finger at Berta.

"Bring her," he orders his henchmen.

"No!" I snarl, stepping in front of Berta. "Leave her the fuck alone."

The muscle-bound henchman I knocked unconscious earlier doesn't break stride as the back of his hand connects with my face. The force of the blow sends my skull cracking into the wall, denting the damp plaster, before my knees buckle.

Berta screams as the muscled beast grabs her by the arm, but not before she clutches hold of my hands. I try to hold onto her, but I can barely focus. As her grip loosens, I feel something hard and cold, something meant to be kept hidden, being forced into my palm. I swallow it with my hands as Berta is dragged out of the room.

"Keep fighting," sneers the blonde as I struggle to stay conscious. "It's amusing to watch you flail."

The three men leave, bolting the door behind them.

———

I spit blood after they leave and look at the gift Berta forced into my hands. It's Lily, the pearl-handled switchblade I keep in my boot. It was a gift from my father when I first left home and a constant companion ever since. Berta must have found it when the dogs were attempting to turn me into a late supper.

Returning it to the moleskin sheath sewn inside my boot, I drag myself over to my coat and search the pockets. The sap is gone, along with Berta's phone. The only thing not missing is the white envelope nestled in an inside pocket.

Curious, I open the envelope to find the two hundred dollars I won on a dog untouched. I'm not sure if that's irony or not, but I stuff it in my back pocket with the thought that only an idiot would think she'll have a chance to spend it.

The rest of my coat is a ruin. The lining is in shreds, the leather is riddled with teeth marks and stained with dog spit, and the awkward zipper down the back has been torn loose. I hate to say it, but it may even be beyond the resurrection skills of Mrs. Pennell's sewing kit.

I want to weep. Not for the coat, but for everything else. How could I have been so stupid as to come here alone? My mouth is bleeding, my head and face are throbbing, and every square inch of flesh is alert with pain. But worst of all, what are they doing to Berta?

I turn to the other women. They've barely moved or said a word. Each one has been given a portable army cot, a blanket, and little else. Their skin is sallow from lack of sunlight and their clothes are a mismatched scatter of thrift store castoffs.

"Where did they take her?" I ask.

The six women stare back in silence.

"Do any of you speak English?"

Nothing but large eyes and slack mouths.

"It's okay," I say, swallowing my frustration. "I'm not one of them. You can see that, right?"

One of the women clears her throat and says, "You bring trouble. We not want trouble."

"Yeah," I sigh, "but that's the problem, isn't it? These bastards have locked you up, forced you to get pregnant, and are doing God knows what with your babies. But you don't want trouble? Trust me, ladies, you're drowning in fucking trouble, and holding your breath in the hope it will get flushed away isn't the answer."

No response.

"Sorry," I add, sighing again. "Who the hell am I to judge, right? You've been locked in here for months and subjected to who knows what brutality. I've only been here a few hours and I can barely stand."

With a groan, I pull myself back onto my feet and attempt to walk around the room. My muscles scream, causing me to stumble and want to give up, but I know I have to stop my legs from seizing up if I'm going to stand any chance of getting out.

As I lumber around the room, I check the lone bathroom—toilet, sink, single shower stall—in the back corner before testing the boards fastened across the three east-facing windows. Despite small gaps that allow some outside light in, none of the boards are loose. Somebody has used quality screws rather than nails.

Peering through one of the larger gaps, I see the glass beyond has been coated in some kind of semi-opaque white wash to stop the curious in nearby buildings from looking in or anyone trying to send an SOS out.

What bothers me most, however, is that—unless the blonde has a permanent repairman on staff—there's no sign that any of these women even tried.

"Are you always kept in this room?" I ask.

The woman who spoke before nods.

"And were you always kept here?"

The woman shakes her head. "Only *wciąży*... err, with baby. We in other rooms before."

"How many rooms?"

The woman shrugs. "Maybe four, maybe more."

"And you're all Polish?"

"No. But all same."

"What does that mean?"

"Not legal. Brought on boat."

I study the faces: all of them far too young and far too broken. They were rounded up and herded into this room as soon as they were pregnant so the majority of the guards could concentrate on the fresh arrivals who still had some fight in them. Once pregnant, they became easier to control because they had something other than their own lives to lose.

"Do the moms who give birth ever come back?" I ask.

The woman looks down and strokes her swollen belly. "We are told that after birth we are free to go."

"And you believe that?"

Tears fall from the woman's eyes, but there's no need to answer. The question wasn't fair.

I want to tell her, tell them all, that I'll get them out of here, that everything will be okay—but I can't. At the moment, I'm as trapped as they are.

———

I return to the wall where my head dented the plaster. Pushing my finger deep into the center of the depression, I'm able to poke through and pull a chunk loose. Beneath the plaster is a series of thin, hardwood boards nailed into the studs. Lathe and plaster. It was a common building method for interior walls before drywall appeared on the scene in the 1950s.

To break through to the next room, I will need to remove the plaster and smash the boards, but that will only get me halfway. I will then need to do the same on the other side of the studs, and chances are good the door is just as locked on that side, too.

Still, the only other option is to give up and that's really not my style.

I'm busy picking away at the plaster when the bolt slides open and the blonde reappears with his henchmen in tow. The muscle-bound ox who I knocked unconscious earlier roars when he sees what a mess I've made of the wall and breaks rank to charge like a rhino with a wasp up its ass.

Instead of cowering in fright like he's expecting, I turn to face him, hoping my muscles are up to the task that my mind is already formulating.

As Pinch has taught me, you can't stop a charging bull, but with the right technique, you can redirect it.

I duck below the gorilla's swiping paw, feeling his hand skim the top of my head as I stab him deep in the kidneys with a straight hand. My other hand, meanwhile, has grabbed his wrist and yanked it closer so that I control his momentum and use his own weight against him.

Before he realizes what I'm doing, the gorilla is spinning past me and straight into one of the boarded-up windows. He bounces off with a splintering of wood and lands on his back.

He barely has time to blink before I land on his chest with both knees, cracking ribs and deflating lungs, and bring my fists to bear. His nose snaps under the first well-aimed blow, spurting blood across his cheek, but I'm stopped before I can add another.

The second henchman grabs me from behind and yanks me, kicking and flailing, off his partner. I'm quickly reduced to squirming and cursing as he holds me aloft and puts his gym membership to good use. My arms, crushed against my sides, lose all feeling as the circulation is cut off, and I find it difficult to breathe as the man squeezes my body like it's an empty toothpaste tube with one last drop trapped in its neck.

When my face turns from purple to blue, the blonde orders the man to release me.

I hit the ground with a thump, thinking I can keep my feet, but I can't. I drop to my knees, sucking in breath and plotting revenge.

The second henchman helps his friend to his feet and they both stare at me like I'm a moldy sandwich at the bottom of the fridge that needs to be disposed of.

"What?" I rasp. "Never been beat up by a girl before?"

The gorilla roars and tries to break free from his partner, but the blonde orders him to stand down.

"Are we quite finished?" the blonde asks.

"I'm not," I say, staring up at the gorilla.

"Look at *me* when I'm talking," says the blonde. "Or I *will* take him off his leash and we'll see just how far that mouth will get you."

I swivel my head and fix my gaze, but the fire in my eyes still burns hot and furious.

"Your man gives good hugs," I say, rubbing the circulation back into my arms. "Real teddy bear."

I hear another growl coming from the henchmen but don't bother displaying any acknowledgment.

"I've been told you were at the shipyard yesterday," says the blonde, "when the cops arrived too late for a barbecue."

My voice is ice. "Are you taking about four dead women in a shipping container? That barbecue?"

"Dead women are no use to me. Graboski was running a shoddy operation and needed a slap. You did me a favor."

"I've been told you don't import. You steal."

"Not true," says the blonde. "I purchase. If the supplier is double-dipping and ripping off his customers by claiming theft, that's his problem."

"And all's fair in blood and profits, right?"

"Who cares about fair?"

"Then what's your interest?"

"The filth. How did they know?"

"If by filth, you mean the cops, then I told them."

"Why did they listen?"

I hesitate, sensing a trap, but it's too late.

"They trust you," he adds, piecing it together himself. "Your Polish friends play neighborhood vigilante and then you call in the clean-up crew. You sleeping with someone? This detective you're always quoting in your stories, Frank Fury?"

"Fuck you."

He laughs. "No judgment. I don't care if you're blowing the whole squad." He reaches into his pocket and produces my phone. "You don't have as many friends as you let on, but I notice there's a Frank listed here. I want you to call him."

I cover my concern with disdain. "Why?"

"You're going to give him a tip."

"About what?"

"A bomb."

"Fuck you."

"We can do that too if you like, although I'd have to tie you down real tight first. I don't mind feisty, but you've got claws."

When I don't rise to the bait, his smile slips. "You'll make the call."

"And if I don't?"

"Do we need to go there?" He waves a dismissive hand at the other women. "You know what I'm capable of."

"What bomb?" I ask.

His smile returns. "That's better. You'll tell Frank that an explosive device is going to be planted in the maternity ward at St. Luke's Women's Center with a detonation target of four p.m. today. After you deliver that message, you will hang up."

"Why do you want to tip him off?"

"That's not your concern."

"Why a maternity ward, then?" I snarl in frustration. "Could you *be* a bigger monster?"

"As you said before, all's fair in blood and profits." He shrugs. "It's business."

"Business?" The gears in my brain are working overtime, then I glance over at the pregnant women. "Supply and demand? You're selling the babies. And what? You don't want the competition? The parents at St. Luke's aren't selling their babies. You're insane."

"Am I?"

I almost gag on my own spit. "Yes!"

"Have you studied adoption rates?"

"What? No."

The cold smile settles upon his lips again. "Private adoption rates in America spike after every headline disaster. The more terrible the tragedy, the better. It's like a drug in the brain. People die and those left living feel a burning need to continue life, to get pregnant or adopt a child. I have a surplus that's eating into profit and this action will create demand. The poor parentless babies who miraculously survive and need a home." His smile widens. "Won't you help the poor orphans?"

I find it difficult to speak as all the saliva has evaporated from my throat. "I've never heard of anything so cruel."

"Then you're clearly not listening." The blonde holds out my phone. "Call Frank. No mistakes. Don't make me cut into my profits any further by gutting one of these women in front of you."

His threat has the desired effect on the women huddled on the bunks as they tremble and wail in fear, and their eyes burn into my skull with pleading desperation.

Still on my knees, I accept the phone with a shaking hand and call up my short contact list.

"Do it," orders the blonde.

I touch the contact and place the phone to my ear.

When the voice answers, I deliver the message. When I hang up, my phone pings and I click the Accept button on the alert that appears on its screen.

The blonde snatches the phone out of my hand. "What was that?"

"Angry Birds," I explain. "New upgrade available."

"Is she mine now?" interrupts the guerrilla with the broken nose and cracked ribs.

"Not yet," snaps the blonde impatiently. He skims the phone, seeing nothing untoward, before taking a small paperclip out of his pocket and using it to expertly eject the phone's SIM card. He snaps the pinkie-nail-sized card in half and drops it in his pocket before tossing the useless phone to me.

I catch it mid-air. "Now that I've done your dirty work, can I see Berta?"

"Not a good idea," says the blonde. "She's a little under the weather."

I rise to my feet, gritting my teeth the whole way. "What have you bastards done to her?"

The two henchmen move forward to block my path to their boss as the blonde turns and exits the room. The gorilla displays bloodied teeth in an open threat before following his partner out the door.

The bolt slides home behind them, and in the newfound silence, I hear the other women weep.

TWENTY-ONE

WITHOUT ITS SIM CARD, the smartphone is useless. No calls in, no calls out, and the only way to use it as a weapon is to force it down somebody's throat and have them choke on it. The thought makes me smile.

I check the boards on the window where the gorilla bounced off. Several of them are cracked, but they resist my attempts to break them any further. Pins and needles run down my weakened arms as I turn my attention back to the room. The women are huddled even closer together than before, as if I'm the young cuckoo who's invaded their nest.

"Do you know anything about his bombs?" I ask.

Their volunteer spokesperson shakes her head.

"Did you know Ania? Ania Zajak?"

The woman shrugs. "She was in other group. We met once before she taken away to give birth."

"He planted a bomb inside her," I say, "after he removed her baby. Did he do that here or does he have access to a medical clinic?"

The woman's eyes grow wide in panic as the other women clutch at each other and start weeping again.

"Sorry," I blurt. "Sorry. Didn't mean to panic anyone, but the reality is this sick fuck has no compunction about doing whatever the hell he wants. The more information I have, the better."

"Why?" asks the woman derisively. "What good does information do you now?"

"I'm shutting him down," I fire back. "But if he's making bombs here, then we're all in even more danger."

The woman sneers at me. "How you shut him down? You trapped here like us."

I glance at the broken boards on the window, wishing I could see outside. "Not for long."

"How?"

A dangerously thin smile creases my lips. "I didn't call Frank."

———

Alone on the other side of the room from my pregnant cellmates, I chew my fingernails to the quick, wincing as each new rip and tear causes pain, and yet unable to stop myself.

I think about Berta and hope she's okay. She's tough, but it's an armored shell that's formed from bad experience and abuse rather than training or confidence. She's tough because she's had to be; not by choice, but as the only way to survive. And while it appears strong, that armor is full of cracks that are easily pried open with

185

the right combination of words or deeds to expose the vulnerable flesh beneath.

The first explosion makes the building shake and the women scream. The sound of automatic gunfire that follows doesn't do anything to ease their fear.

"Get in the corner!" I yell as I rush toward the bolted door. "And keep your heads down."

I press myself to the wall beside the door and remove the knife from my boot. With the blade open, I wait, listening to the chaos as it climbs the stairs and enters the hallway outside.

White smoke trickles underneath the door and the sound of gunfire is punctuated by grunts, screams, and cries of both pain and confusion.

When the gunfire dies, I slap my hand against the solid door and call out. "In here."

A muffled voice calls back. "You alone?"

"Me and six prisoners," I call back. "No guards."

The bolt thunders back and the door swings open, causing a thick cloud of white smoke to pour into the room.

Through the smoke, the red-hot tip of a compact submachine gun enters the room first. It's followed by a short, stout, heavily-armed soldier dressed in black body armor complete with a half-face filtration mask, oversized goggles, and Kevlar helmet. All he needs is a colorful bandanna and he could be one of the Mutant Ninja Turtles.

"Thanks for coming," I say, coughing slightly at the smoke. "Sorry about the bouncers. They're a bit overzealous."

Pinch swivels his head to see me pressed against the wall. He pulls downs his respirator and smiles as if I've just popped out of a birthday cake.

"They let you keep your knife?" he asks. "Standards have slipped."

Sliding the blade back into its handle, I rush forward to give him an extra-hard squeeze, surprising myself with the flood of emotion that threatens to overwhelm me.

"I wasn't sure if you would know what I was asking," I blubber. "They were monitoring every word."

"Calling me Frank helped, especially since I could tell you weren't drunk dialing."

We both laugh as I quickly bring Pinch up to speed on the situation.

"We do need to call Frank," I say. "This building has six floors. The freak in charge is a bomb maker and could have explosives planted anywhere. I also don't know how many women are imprisoned here."

Pinch hands me a disposable phone. "I noticed your signal went dead shortly after the call."

"The alert you sent spooked him."

"Sorry, I needed your GPS coordinates."

"Don't apologize," I say with a smile. "I tried not to let it show, but I was completely out of options." I turn to indicate the huddle of women. "Even these nice gals were questioning my sanity."

Pinch laughs again, but then stops abruptly at the sound of panicked voices echoing in the hallway, demanding a response from the floor's guards. Pinch slides his respirator in place and disappears back into the smoke. A few seconds later, an angry burst of machine-gun fire is followed by the roar of a shotgun and yelling voices. A second burst of machine-gun fire is followed by silence.

Pinch returns through the smoke and lifts his mask.

"Make your call," he says. "Staying here isn't safe."

I dial Frank's number. He answers on the third ring.

"It's Dixie," I say. "I've found your bomber, but it's all kicking off. You need to bring SWAT, ambulances, and the bomb squad."

I hold the phone away from my ear for a moment while Frank sputters an impressive litany of profanity.

"I'll apologize later," I interrupt, "but I need you down here now. There are dozens of women in need of care and a building full of armed assholes. I'm going to try to get the women outside. I need you there to meet us."

I give him the address and hang up before Frank can protest further. When I go to hand the phone back, Pinch tells me to keep it or toss it. Either way, it's useless to him.

I turn and lob it to the pregnant women in the corner in case any of them have family in the area. Not one of them has moved an inch since Pinch appeared out of the smoke.

"Stay here," I tell them, "until we can escort you out. If any of the guards come while we're gone, scream as loud as you can."

When I turn back, Pinch hands me a Beretta semi-automatic handgun and an extra ammunition clip.

"I want that gun back later," he says with a wink. "Smoke is lifting. Stay behind me and let's clear this floor."

In the hallway, I gather my bearings and point to a closed door on our left.

"That's his office," I say. "The bastard in charge."

"What do you know about him?"

"He has two dogs, a cruel streak, and likes torturing women. He took my friend to keep me in line."

"I don't like dogs," says Pinch. "They don't know when to back down." He glances over his shoulder at my bandaged arm and leg. "They do that?"

I nod. "But maybe they won't attack if he can't give the order."

The stern look on Pinch's face says to wipe the thought from my mind. "Don't hesitate," he says. "They're trained not to. Are all the women friendlies?"

I nod.

"That makes it easier. Kill all the men. We'll let God sort them out upstairs."

The moment we enter the room, the dogs attack in perfect, uniform silence like the raptors in *Jurassic Park*. We stop them before they reach us.

Unfortunately, the rest of the room is empty. No sign of the blonde or Berta.

"Clear?" asks Pinch.

"Clear," I respond with heavy heart.

"Keep it together," orders Pinch. "We'll find your friend."

Pinch and I return to the hallway and cautiously make our way down its length with him ordering me to keep alert for any movement behind us in case reinforcements descend from the floors above.

The air is thick with the metallic tang of cordite, and the linoleum is slick with pools of dark liquid leaking from the bodies of six guards that Pinch dispatched earlier, but there's no more resistance as we unbolt the doors and check each of the remaining rooms.

Apart from the first two rooms at the mouth of the hallway that were used by the blonde and his guards as offices, the remainder of the rooms are holding cells for women in the first two stages of their profitability cycle: sex and babies.

In each room, I talk to the women, reassuring them that we're going to get them to safety. I also ask about Berta, but the answer is always the same: no one has seen her.

"What now?" Pinch asks as we clear the last room.

"We need to get outside," I say. "It's too risky to move up to the other floors. Frank will be here soon with the heavy equipment, but we can get these women out first."

"And your friend?"

I swallow and make the difficult decision. "She'll need to wait. I made these women a promise."

"Round them up," says Pinch. "I'll make sure no one comes down from upstairs."

As Pinch rushes up the hallway toward the main staircase, I return to each room and ask the women to follow me. The last room I enter is the first one I was thrown into.

"Ready to go?" I ask the six women.

"This is not trick?" asks the spokesperson.

"Look at me," I say with a half-hearted smile. "All I want is a bath and a very large drink, and unless you've been holding out on me, you've got neither of those things here. I'm going home. You want to come?"

The woman rises to her feet and is quickly joined by the other five.

"You are unusual woman, Dixie Flynn."

"Oh, sweetie," I sigh. "You don't know the half of it."

———

When I join Pinch at the mouth of the hallway, I have close to forty terrified women lined up behind me.

"Anything?" I ask, peering over his shoulder at the staircase.

"Lots of noise, but nobody's tried to come down. Could be building barricades, planning to make a stand."

"Not our war," I say. "Not this time."

I signal the women to begin making their way down, but before half of them have made it into the stairwell, a loud, terrified scream from below stops them cold.

Cursing, I immediately push past the row of women to descend the stairs toward the origin of the scream. As I turn the last bend, I see one of the pregnant women being held on her tiptoes by the gorilla.

He's bleeding from a serious chest wound and a large gash across his forehead, but he's still got enough strength to hold the woman's neck in one hand and a revolver in the other. The gun is pressed against the woman's temple and together they're blocking the only exit out of the building.

When the gorilla sees my face rounding the bend, his upper lip curls into an angry sneer.

I hold up my left hand in a stop motion and say, "It's over. Let us pass."

"Fuck you it's over."

"Your friends are dead. You don't want to join them."

He presses the gun harder against the woman's pale flesh. Its hammer is cocked, his finger on the trigger. "Go back to your rooms," he yells at the women. "All of you."

"We're not doing that," I say. "We're leaving."

"Not while I'm on guard."

With a loud moan of despair, the hostage's water breaks, splashing the floor and soaking the guard's feet. Surprised, the gorilla glances down and snarls.

When he looks back up, I have the Beretta aimed at his face, and before he can react, I squeeze the trigger.

It's not like the movies, all clean and precise—mostly because I miss the forehead shot by a good four inches.

Instead, the bullet explodes inside his mouth, spraying chunks of cheek, teeth, ear, and jawbone across the door to the adjoining room. The fright is too much for the hostage, who faints and becomes dead weight, slipping out of the guard's arms. I yell for him to drop the gun.

Staring up at me, the right side of his face in utter ruin, the gorilla roars in both frustration and agony before turning his gun toward me.

I'm squeezing the trigger again when two bullets zip past my left ear to remove the top of the gorilla's head. My bullet misses, smashing the doorframe as the gorilla's lifeless body drops to the floor.

"Move it!" Pinch screams from a few stairs above me, spurring the shocked women to get in motion again and burst through the front door.

As a couple of us help the limp hostage to her feet and guide her outside, I feel Pinch touch my arm and remove the gun from my hand.

The black SWAT van roars around the corner as we pour into the deserted street, and Pinch whispers in my ear before vanishing into the early dawn.

TWENTY-TWO

THE SWAT TEAM SCREAMS at us to clear the street and move toward the temporary command station being erected at the end of the block. Some of the women decide to take their chances by breaking ranks and fleeing in the opposite direction, but those who have been in custody the longest are too weak and confused to run.

Sticking close to the building, I lead the ragtag group toward the officers who are busy erecting barricades and moving the command vehicle into position. On the other side of the barricade, several ambulances pull up and EMTs rush out to help.

"You'll need to call for a bigger bus," I tell one of the paramedics, a young woman in her early twenties who hands me a soft blue blanket to wrap myself in. "These women need fluids and proper care. Half of them are pregnant."

When Frank approaches, he's in no mood to banter.

"She alright?" he asks the paramedic.

"I haven't examined her yet, but those injuries look severe."

"I'm fine," I say. "*And* I'm standing right here."

"You don't look fine," says Frank.

"Your leg is bleeding," adds the paramedic. "The bandage is a mess. And your face! Who did that?"

"I'll come back after I've talked with this grump. A friend of mine is still inside that building."

Frank takes me by the arm, his grip rougher than normal. "What the hell?" he snarls. "I thought we agreed you were going to call me *before* you got into this kind of trouble."

"It happened too fast," I say. "Berta called to say she spotted the bomber and planned to follow him. I rushed down here before she got in trouble, but I was too late. He'd already grabbed her."

"Berta?"

"A friend. She's the one who's still trapped inside. I couldn't call you because I didn't know she was inside until I took a look, but when I took a look, they grabbed me, too."

Frank leads me into the command vehicle and closes the door. "Tell me everything. Start at the beginning and don't leave out a single detail."

I tell him everything. Well, almost everything. I leave out any mention of Pinch, which makes it awkward to explain how I managed to escape. And although Frank doesn't appear to wholly buy my lie of an unexpected attack by a rival gang, neither does he bother questioning it. For now.

"And you're sure it's the same guy from the composite I showed you?" he asks.

"Positive, but he never gave me his name."

Frank's eyes shift slightly and I can tell he's holding something back.

"You know who he is?" I ask.

"We received a hit back from Scotland Yard. His name is Eldred Jacks. He operated a trafficking ring in England that specialized in bringing sex workers into the country and moving money out."

"And?" I press, sensing more.

"He was arrested two years ago while escorting two women over to the Caymans. Both women were pretending to be pregnant."

"Pretending?"

"They were wearing fake pregnancy bellies stuffed with cash. The prosthetics were state of the art, but not perfect. Jacks walked on the charges as both women denied knowing him."

My face pales as I remember my conversation with Ania and her comment that her raw scar was "one of many."

"He's still doing it, isn't he?" I say. "Except instead of prosthetics, he's using real pregnant women. That's what gave him the idea to put the bomb inside Ania."

Frank's eyes harden. "Homeland Security arrested a woman at the airport this morning. I only received the report on my way over here. Because of the bombing, pregnant women—especially one traveling alone—jumped to the top of their list. She had a cesarian scar and a preliminary exam failed to register a heartbeat."

"Jesus!"

"She was escorted to hospital, where an X-ray revealed she was carrying bundles of cash instead of a baby."

"That fucking monster!"

"She's having it removed now, but we managed to get a copy of the composite over to her before the procedure started and she positively identified Eldred Jacks."

I shake my head in disbelief. "He buys the women and forces them into sex slavery, making sure they don't use protection, which in this sick day and age probably makes them more valuable. When they get pregnant, he sells the babies and then forces the women to traffic money out of the country inside their bodies. How many times can he do that before it kills them?"

"I wondered that, too," says Frank. "I've got the coroner looking into some of our recent Jane Does now to see if any of them had cesareans."

"It ends here, Frank," I say, rising to my feet. "You need to get Berta out of there and burn that fucking building down to the ground with him in it."

"I'll bring in my team," says Frank. "And you can tell us everything you know about what's going on inside. The place is surrounded. Trust me, nobody's getting out."

———

After I explain as much as I know about the interior of the building, Frank has Detective Shaw escort me back to an ambulance to be checked over by the young paramedic. Her name turns out to be Shirley Johnstone and she's a fan of my work, which makes me like her even more.

When she unwraps the bandage from my leg, Shirley wrinkles her nose. "You need stitches and a rabies shot. I'd also recommend a treatment of antibiotics to prevent infection."

"Can you do the stitches here?" I ask, glancing over at the building. "I don't want to leave my friend."

"Lucky for you, I'm Level Three." Shirley smiles. "But you have to promise not to bitch about the scar. I haven't done that many field operations."

"You have to be better than my last surgeon." I show her the vivid scar across the center of my palm. "She was a coroner. No bedside manner at all."

Shirley chuckles and retrieves her full medical kit. "This will hurt," she says. "I need to flush the wound, then inject local anesthetic before stitching."

"No problem. Just give me a scotch first will you? I've had a bitch of a morning."

Shirley laughs again. "Sorry, only the driver has keys to the bar."

I turn to Shaw. "What about you? Got a flask hidden in that jacket somewhere?"

"How can you joke?" he snaps. "You've set off a powder keg here and men are putting their lives at risk. For what?"

"For what?" I snap back. "Look at these women huddled around you. Those blankets are the first touch of warmth they've had in God knows how long. They were shipped over here in horrendous conditions, sold into slavery, forced to have sex with strangers, and then herded like cattle into pens until they were ready to give birth. Yeah, the situation is FUBAR, but I'm not the one to blame here."

Shaw doesn't back down. "We would have caught him. On our terms, with less risk."

"Well tough titties," I spit. "Those women couldn't wait to fit into your goddamn schedule. You've got him cornered now, so quit whining about procedure and finish the damn job."

With a snarl, Shaw turns heel and stomps away.

"Sheesh," says Shirley. "I wish the bar *was* open. Even I could use a drink after that."

I wince as she flushes the wound and applies the first stab of anesthetic, but I allow the pain to focus my mind and brace myself for the onslaught to come.

If life has taught me anything, it's that monsters like Eldred Jacks never go quietly.

———

When I'm stitched up and properly bandaged—my chew-toy of an arm needing needle and thread, too—the biggest pain is in my left butt cheek where the rabies shot came in a needle large enough to make me feel faint.

With a slight limp, I return to the command vehicle and knock on the door.

Frank allows me entry despite the vocal protest of the younger detective.

"She's the only one who's been inside," Frank growls at him. "We might need that."

Four video monitors show a live feed from helmet cams mounted on lead members of the SWAT team, while a set of speakers fills the cabin with official chatter. On the monitors, I recognize the first floor hallway that Pinch cleared before we led the women to safety. There are at least six dead bodies on the floor and dozens of bare footprints smearing the blood. Since they were never allowed to leave the building, none of the women had shoes.

"Any resistance?" I ask.

Frank shakes his head. "Somebody beat us to it. Your rival gang theory, I'm guessing."

"The guy in the front entrance was missing most of his head," adds Shaw with a condescending sneer. "Some real animals at work there. Surprised they just disappeared and let you walk out."

"Yeah," I fire back. "It would have been so much better if they'd decided to rape us all first."

Shaw's cheeks redden as Frank taps one of the monitors that shows a team member entering an empty room with two dead dogs on the ground. "Who kills a dog?" he asks.

"That was his office," I explain. "The bomber. Jacks. Those were his attack dogs. Misch and Hentschel."

"Huh," says Frank. "Those were the names of Hitler's personal bodyguards."

I wince. "Charming."

Frank picks up the mike and relays the information to the SWAT commander.

"Floor's clear." The commander's voice echoes over the speakers. "Preparing to move up."

"Be careful," I say aloud, despite knowing he can't hear me, which only makes Shaw's Evil Eye intensify.

My heart is in my throat as I watch the monitors, and then all hell breaks loose as a barrage of gunfire from the third landing sends the team scrambling.

"Shit!" screams Shaw behind me. "How many men does he have up there?"

"I don't know! I only saw his two henchmen, but I don't think he has many. That's why he ran."

It's difficult to monitor exactly what is happening as the four head cams swivel, duck, and dive, but a return volley of gunfire is quickly followed by smoke grenades and flash-bangs as the police squad rushes the improvised barricade at the top of the stairs.

It's over within seconds, and two more members of Jacks's gang lie silently bleeding while the barricade is torn asunder. Apart from the two dead guards, the rest of the floor appears deserted. Two of the rooms have been converted into a bordello-style lounge area with couches, floor rugs, a stand-up bar, and even an old piano. The other rooms are strictly business: single beds, dim lighting, and cheap curtains over the boarded-up windows to make them look less like prison cells.

None of the rooms are occupied.

"There's an elevator," I tell Frank. "He must use it to bring clients directly to the second floor."

Frank passes on the information and I watch the monitor as one of the officers presses the button for the elevator and covers its door with his weapon. The clockwork dial above the door shows the elevator rising from ground level.

When the doors open, the elevator is empty, but it makes me wonder if Jacks used it to escape.

The third and fourth floors show no sign of occupation, and the only movement is from a family of rats that scatter when the SWAT teams lobs a smoke grenade in their direction.

The top floor is less decrepit than the two below it, but not by much. When the squad uncovers evidence of bomb-making equipment in the first room, the atmosphere inside the van grows heavier.

"No babies," I say, cracking the silence. "Where's he keeping the babies?"

"No sign of him either," says Frank.

"Or Berta."

The speakers crackle with panic and the monitor feed is a jumble of movement as the commander barks orders for his squad to evacuate. Frank snaps up the mike and asks for a situation report.

"Trip wire," yells the commander as he pounds down the stairs, surrounded by his squad. "Stay back."

His words are barely out of the speakers when a loud explosion rocks the van.

"Damnit!" Frank yells as I sprint for the door.

I'm the first outside to witness the top floor of the building spewing a thick cloud of bricks and dust. Seconds later, broken red bricks begin dropping from the sky like murderous rain.

"Take cover!" I yell as I push back into the van, causing Frank to stagger backward, cracking Shaw on the nose with his elbow and dropping the younger man to the floor.

"Bricks," I say, pointing skyward just before the sound of them denting and bouncing off the roof punctuates my point.

Shaw pulls himself off the floor with a glower that says it's all my fault.

I don't bother to argue.

———

Apart from one twisted knee and a dented helmet, all members of the SWAT team make it out of the building in one piece.

After he finishes talking with Frank, I approach the SWAT commander to ask about Berta.

He shakes his head. "We searched every floor except for the back half of the top one. There was no sign of anyone else inside."

"Are there other exits?"

"The place is a rat's nest, ma'am. I'd guess there are quite a few. Now if you'll excuse me, I still have work to do."

I look down at my feet, worrying about Berta. When I lift my head again, Frank is by my side.

"You look like shit," he says. "Why don't you go home?"

"I must look bad," I agree. "Your SWAT guy just called me ma'am."

Frank has difficulty keeping a smile off his face, but he keeps it in check.

"The chief has authorized the distribution of the composite. It'll be all over the morning news. Jacks won't get far."

"I was told last night that he has an apartment near here." I point up the street. "Back that way somewhere. I don't have an address."

"We'll get him."

"In time?" I snap.

Frank's eyes harden again. "What do you mean, *in time?*"

"Shit, Frank." I pinch the bridge of my nose, my voice quivering with panic. "When Jacks was holding me hostage, he wanted me to call you with a tip."

"What kind of tip?"

"A bomb. He wanted me to tell you he was planting a bomb at St. Luke's Women's Center. In the maternity ward. He said it would detonate at four p.m. today."

"And you're just telling me this now?"

"I thought we had him trapped," I say. "But even now, it doesn't make sense. Why did he want me to alert you?"

"With Homeland Security involved, he knew we'd take it damn seriously," says Frank.

"Which would also make it a good distraction," I say. "Get the cops looking in one direction while he takes off in another. A flight to the Caymans, maybe."

"We'll check out St. Luke's to be safe, but the sooner we nab this prick the better." Frank sighs and looks around. "There's nothing more for you to do here, Dix. Go home, get some rest, and I'll be in touch."

"Somehow I get the feeling you're just tired of seeing my face."

"You have looked better," he quips dryly before jabbing a thumb over his shoulder. "The media is corralled down that way. I'd prefer if you went the other."

"That bad, huh?"

Frank fixes me with a solemn stare. "The less the brass knows about your involvement here, the fewer questions I need to ask about what really happened inside."

"I already told you—"

Frank shakes his head to cut me off. "We got a deal?"

I look over my shoulder at the direction Frank wants me to go. "Any taxi stands down that way? My phone's broken."

Frank digs in his pocket and pulls out some loose change. "If anyone can find one, Dix, it's you. If not," he hands me two quarters, "use a pay phone."

"You're a big softie at heart, Frank."

"For now," he says. "But if Forensics tells me you killed any of those men, it'll be a different story. No matter how much they may deserve it, I won't support crossing that line. Now go."

With one final look at the smoking building where I last saw Berta alive, I hobble away.

TWENTY-THREE

I creep into my building, not wanting to disturb any of my neighbors and have them witness the state I'm in, and head directly upstairs to my apartment.

Inside, four yellow balloons are floating close to the ceiling like a forgotten birthday bouquet.

"What the hell?" I say aloud as Prince pops his head out of the bedroom before rushing over to rub against my legs. He prefers the bandaged bare leg to the one still covered in half a pair of jeans. Since I haven't shaved in a while, it gives him a better scratch.

Reaching down gingerly, I scoop the orange furball into my arms, raising him to my face and laughing as he gently places a paw on my cheek and licks my nose. His rough tongue is the kindest of kisses that unlocks a dam in my eyes.

I move to the couch to sit for awhile and cry.

When my body stops shaking and my eyes are raw, I head to the bathroom, strip off, and step into the tub. Having been told not to get my bandages wet, I run warm water without the drain plug and awkwardly clean myself with a wet cloth.

In the bedroom, I examine myself in the mirror. Ribs are tender but not broken, face is bruised and swollen, arms and the length of my back are a mottled kaleidoscope of ugly hues from fending off advances from vicious pricks in both canine and human form.

With a sigh, I glance at the clock. It's barely seven in the morning. The newsroom will be deserted unless some eager beaver got wind of the siege on Jacks's building. I could break the story on the web and annoy the hell out of the breakfast TV newscasts once again, but my head is fuzzy and I don't have the confidence that I can distinguish between the lies I told and the truth that needs telling.

My unmade bed and the crumpled pile of soft, warm pajamas calls to me. For extra incentive, Prince jumps onto the pile and starts kneading the baggy cotton bottoms. *Mmmmm*, he purrs, *comfy*.

I laugh at the voice I've created in my head for him. It has a slight, Scottish lilt. Where did that come from?

Despite the near-impossible-to-resist invitation, I ease into a fresh pair of jeans, clean shirt, and socks before returning to the kitchen to brew a pot of strong coffee.

I'm taking the first sip when a new yellow object appears on the ceiling. This time, the balloon is only half inflated but growing larger, its stem protruding from the bullet hole in the ceiling that I never got around to repairing.

My anger flares as I dash to the gun safe in my bedroom closet, pull out the Governor, and dart back. As soon as the balloon is fully inflated and released into the room, I aim the Governor at the hole and squeeze the button on its grip. The crimson laser fires along the length of the barrel and enters the hole.

A male voice cries out, "Woah!" from the room above.

"Who's there?" I yell up at the ceiling. "Get your ass down here now or I'll riddle you and your floor with more holes."

"Coming," says the voice. "Don't shoot."

I unlock the front door and move into a position to cover it with my gun. When the knock comes, I tell him to enter. The sight is nothing like I expect.

Wearing baggy yellow pantaloons covered in a rainbow of colored circles, striped knee-high socks, and a plain white T-shirt covered in lipstick kisses and matching red suspenders, the man is a clown—or at least, half a clown. The white pancake on his face is blotchy and smeared, his bulbous red nose is missing and his short black hair looks like it's normally kept under a crazy wig. Beneath the botched makeup, however, he's actually kinda cute.

When he spots the gun, he raises his hands in surrender.

"Who the hell are you?" I ask.

He gulps. "Your new neighbor? I just moved in."

"And what are you? A clown?"

"Children's entertainer, actually."

"Why are you shoving balloons through the hole in my ceiling?"

His cheeks flush red beneath the smeared pancake. "I thought it would be a fun way to introduce myself."

"And how do you know I didn't shoot the last neighbor who tried to be funny? Maybe that's where the hole came from in the first place."

"Uh." He gulps again. "Uh. Kristy, your friend, told me the hole was an accident and that you were actually, kinda, you know, nice."

"Kristy thinks everyone's nice. What's your name?"

"My friends call me Bubbles."

This makes me smile. "That's the name of my pet goldfish."

"Really? Do you still have him?"

"Prince ate him."

His eyes widen in alarm. "Who's Prince?"

"My vicious, overprotective, and very jealous," I pause for effect, "kitten."

The first smile ripples across his lips. "I see."

"He doesn't appreciate your balloons."

"Sorry. Didn't mean to step on his turf."

Sensing he's harmless, I lower the gun. "Coffee? I just brewed a pot."

"That would be great," he says. "Bit of a long night, actually."

"At a children's party?" I enter the kitchenette and grab a second mug.

His cheeks flush crimson again. "I also do the occasional bachelorette gig."

"As a clown?"

He shrugs. "Some ladies love it. I bust a mean move in my oversized clown shoes."

I smirk. "I bet you do."

He joins me in the kitchen. "I also DJ and juggle, do lame magic tricks, tell jokes. Keeps people entertained."

I notice his eyes being drawn to the nearly-complete hangman puzzle on the counter, and have to ask, "You haven't been sending me red parcels as well, have you?"

"No. Why?"

I indicate the puzzle. "Somebody's sending me pieces of that puzzle. One piece every day."

"Sorry, I don't know anything about it, but that's way creepier than balloons."

I hand him his coffee and indicate that we should sit on the couch.

After we sit, Prince strolls out of the bedroom and jumps on one of the chairs beside us. He stares at Bubbles intently for a few moments before lifting his leg and licking his privates.

"Neat trick," says Bubbles. "If I could do that, the bachelorettes would go wild."

I burst out laughing.

"Probably get bigger tips, too," he adds.

I laugh harder, but have to stop as pain shoots through my ribs.

"You okay?"

"Fine. Just a long night like you said."

He indicates my bruised cheek. "And that?"

"Minor disagreement. It's settled now."

"Kristy told me you were a bit of a trouble magnet."

I smirk. "You and her been gossiping?"

"Nah. She's just filling me in on the neighbors. Sounds like an interesting bunch."

"It's a family," I say. "We look out for each other."

"I like that. The best families are always the ones we build one friend at a time."

He's got a lovely smile and for a few moments I allow myself to relax and bathe in the comfort of frivolous conversation.

After a second cup of coffee, the phone rings and Stoogan's voice blares into the answering machine.

"Damnit, Dix. You're not answering your cell. Pick up, will you? The police are releasing details on your bomber. It's all over the morning news."

"I better call him back," I tell Bubbles.

"Sounds urgent."

"That's just my boss. Man's been breathing deadlines for so long he's in a perpetual panic. That's why there's so few old journalists— our hearts give out before we ever learn to relax."

Bubbles stands up to leave. "Well, if you ever want to chill out or have a laugh, I'm upstairs." He points at the hole in the ceiling. "Just send up a flare."

I laugh and show him to the door.

———

After talking to Stoogan, I head to a local phone store and purchase a new SIM card. It only takes a few minutes for the young tech to work his magic and link my existing number to the new card. My cell then comes back online to inform me that I've missed six calls: two from Frank and four from Stoogan.

I listen to the messages, but none of them are relevant anymore. I call Frank. It takes six rings before he answers.

"Any update on Berta or Jacks?" I ask.

"Nothing yet, although we found Jacks's apartment. It was just a place to crash. Nothing there apart from some questionable jacking-off material."

"Are you looking into the babies? Jacks told me he had a surplus, which means he must have a nursery somewhere."

"We're looking into everything." Frank's tone is harsher than usual.

"You OK?" I ask, concerned.

"I'm great," he snarls. "Media thinks I'm some modern-age crusader, busting two sex slavery rings in two days, why wouldn't I be okay?"

"So what's the problem?" I snap back.

"Explaining it," says Frank. "It's a fucking nightmare."

"Send Shaw out to pick up some breakfast. You're always cranky when your blood sugar drops."

There's a pause and then Frank's familiar chortle. "That's your answer for everything, isn't it? Eat."

"Not for everything, but in this case it'll help. Call me if you get any leads on Berta."

"Yeah. Gotta go."

My next call is to Dr. Irena Krawiec.

When she answers, I say, "I'm coming over. You gonna be there?"

"*Tak*. Yes."

"Have you heard from Berta today?"

"No. Why?"

"I'll tell you when I get there."

———

The taxi drops me in front of the divided mansion in the Richmond District and I make my way to the top floor. When Irena opens the door, she takes one look at me and gasps.

"Who did that?"

"It's OK. He got worse."

She smirks. "Of that I have no doubt, but fighting? You will never find nice boy to settle down if you're bruised all the time."

"Darn, that's where I've been going wrong."

Irena's smirk widens into a grin. "Come in. Tell me everything. Why you asking about Berta?"

Inside, I give her the highlights. When I'm done, she asks, "How many women were there?"

"Close to forty. Some were taken to the hospital, but others, those who were still able, took off."

Irena nods. "I'll make some calls. Let people know to keep eyes open. The poor souls will be lost out there, but they'll find their way to us eventually."

"It's Berta who concerns me the most."

"You believe this Jacks person took her?"

"Only explanation."

"For what reason?"

"I don't know, but there's no good answers. Have you heard of any illegal nurseries where he might be keeping the babies?"

Irena shakes her head. "If I did, we would have tried to shut him down before this."

"When we first met, you had concerns about Polish girls going missing, but you also hinted that fewer women were using your services. Could Jacks have been persuading them to go full-term and give their babies up for private adoption rather than aborting them?"

"Anything's possible, but I never saw—" She stops talking and we both have the same thought at the same time.

"The woman in blue," I say. I remember the pink card she gave me with the baby and stork printed on it, but I left it in either my wrecked jacket or my ruined pants. "When does she usually start harassing your patients?"

"She's here every day," says Irena.

I rush to the front window and look down at the street, trying to peer into the shadows where I remember her lurking. There's no sign of her.

"When she arrives, I need to talk to her," I say, my thoughts firing on all cylinders. "We don't have time to be nice. If she knows where the babies are being kept, we need to get there fast. Berta could be there."

"What do you want me to do?" asks Irena.

"We need muscle."

Irena smiles. "I'll call Jakub. He's a good boy."

———

When Jakub pulls up in his Thunder Gray Cadillac, I step onto the mansion's wide staircase and head down the stairs to meet him. As I walk, I keep my head lowered and my shoulders hunched as though carrying a great burden.

On cue, the lady in blue appears at the foot of the stairs with a pamphlet and a pink business card.

"Bless you, child," she says, "but there are other ways."

I lift my chin and fix my gaze on hers. "And that's exactly what I want to talk to you about."

Before she has any chance to voice alarm, Jakub's large hand engulfs the woman's face while his other arm wraps around her chest and lifts her off the ground.

"Take her up to your aunt's," I say. "We'll talk there."

With the woman squirming uselessly in his arms, Jakub heads inside the mansion. After making sure nobody else is paying attention, I quickly follow.

At the top of the stairs, Irena leads Jakub not into her apartment but to the left, into what turns out to be her operating room.

"Strap her to table," she says.

When Jakub releases his hold on the woman's mouth, Irena immediately stuffs a wad of bandage in it as a gag.

"Don't struggle," she tells the woman in blue. "I've had the clinic sound-proofed, so nobody can hear you."

The woman's eyes are practically bulging out of her head by the time Jakub finishes securing her to the table. Wide leather straps anchor her wrists, while a second pair hold her ankles in stainless steel stirrups.

Irena turns to me and in fake sotto voce asks, "Should I cut off one of her fingers to start, so she knows we're serious?"

"I was thinking a toe," I say, playing along, "but let's see how cooperative she wants to be first."

When Irena removes the gag, the woman, who heard every word, makes a low keening sound in the back of her throat. The array of gynecological instruments and the vulnerable position she's trapped in are enough to terrify anyone.

"The organization you work for," I begin, "have you ever been to the building where they keep the pregnant women?"

The woman in blue swallows before burbling, "Please don't hurt me. I have an invalid husband at home and he's useless without me. I'll tell you anything you want."

"Good. This doesn't have to be painful. We only want straight answers. Have you ever been to the building where they keep the pregnant women?"

She jiggles her chin. "They gave me a tour of the house. It is very nice. Six bedrooms, all with attached bathrooms, and lovely decor."

"Were there any expectant mothers there at the time?"

"No. Not when I was there. It was all very new."

"What about the births? Where are they being done?"

"The house is set up for deliveries. Each room is also a birthing room with round-the-clock doulas, but if there are any complications, there is an arrangement with the hospital."

"And you know this how?"

"They told me."

"Have you ever witnessed a birth there?"

"I have no reason to. What is this? Why did you grab me?"

"The babies," I say, ignoring her questions. "Do you know where they keep the babies?"

"They don't keep the babies. Couples are chosen before the birth so the birth mother can meet the parents of her child. It creates a wonderful bond."

"And you've witnessed this?"

"No, but I can assure you—"

"How?" I snap. "If you haven't witnessed it, how can you assure me of anything?"

"I-I-I—"

"Why did you choose to target this clinic?"

"I-I didn't. It was assigned to me." She looks up at Irena with pleading eyes. "I've always tried to be respectful."

"Who gave you the job?" I ask.

"The reverend, of course."

"Describe him."

"Uh, well, he's, umm, average height, blonde hair, a sharp nose and a rather large birthmark on his left cheek, but—"

"English accent?"

"Yes." She smiles. "It's very pleasant to the ear."

"I take it you don't watch the morning news."

"No." She scrunches her nose. "Too unpleasant."

"Did the reverend take you anyplace other than this home?"

"No, that's all I needed to see. It's really such a wonderful org—"

"I need the address," I interrupt.

The woman swallows again. "And then you'll let me go?"

"We'll untie you and you can go next door with the doctor for a nice cup of tea until such time as we don't need you anymore. How's that?"

"This is all very strange. There was no need to grab me. I have nothing to hide."

"Watch the news," I snap. "Address?"

She gives me the address. It's not far away.

———

"Now what?" asks Jakub after the woman in blue has been escorted back to Irena's apartment.

"Drop me off near the address, then leave. You were never here."

"You sure? I can help."

"I know, but I can't risk Berta's life by going in half-cocked. This needs to be done legit."

"That doesn't sound like you."

"Ha, ha," I say dryly. "You don't know me well enough to be a smartass yet."

Jakub flashes a toothy grin.

———

In the Cadillac, I phone Frank. Six rings, then, "What? I got nothing to share yet."

"I have a lead on Jacks. He's got a clinic operating in the Richmond District, some kind of birthing house. I'm heading there now."

"Damnit, Dix!"

"I'm not going inside; that's why I called. I need your help." I give him the address.

"Stay clear," orders Frank. "If he's inside, you don't want to spook him. I'm looking it up on the computer. OK, there's a coffee shop two blocks away. I'll meet you there."

I hang up and tell Jakub where to drop me.

———

When Frank arrives, he's accompanied by a half-dozen SWAT guys and Detective Shaw.

"This is all you brought?" I ask.

"It's a residential neighborhood," says Frank. "Better to go low-key. What do you know about the place?"

I tell him everything the lady in blue told me.

Detective Shaw places a laptop on the table and pulls up a satellite view of the neighborhood. With a couple of clicks, the image zooms in to show an aerial view of the house.

"Is this a live feed?" I ask.

"No," says Shaw with a mocking grin. "Google Maps. Probably a year old, but it shows us there's a back alley, small rear yard, and a single garage."

"We'll clear the garage first," says Frank. He points to four of the SWAT members. "You four take the rear. Once the garage is clear, we'll move in the front door and you take the back. You know who we're looking for, but there could also be civilians, possibly children."

"And what do I do?" I ask.

"You've already done it," says Frank.

"Hell, no!"

Frank shuts me down with a look. "Don't make me cuff you to this table. Once the house is secure, you can come in to see if your friend is there, but this is no time for amateurs."

I point at Shaw. "Then why are you taking him?"

The six SWAT guys grin, which, selfishly, makes me feel slightly better.

TWENTY-FOUR

I GIVE THE SQUAD a thirty-second head start before I leave the coffee shop and follow. The four guys responsible for the rear of the house take a black van into the alley, while Frank, Shaw, and the remaining two SWAT officers move down the sidewalk. Their formation is tight, like four legs of the same animal, although Shaw is visibly nervous and seems just a half-step off.

I follow Frank's crew, keeping a discreet distance behind them, not wanting my impatience to jeopardize Berta's safety.

When the four men stop one house away from the target, I'm a half-block back. Frank glances in my direction, but his face reveals nothing. As he talks into his radio, one of the SWAT guys opens a black gym bag he's been carrying over his shoulder and removes a steel battering ram from inside. It's smaller than I expect: half the length of a baseball bat, but as wide as an old-fashioned stovepipe.

Frank taps the man on the shoulder as a signal to get ready. When he taps again, all four rush forward in a tight cluster. I sprint to catch up, but my stitched leg makes it more of a cumbersome three-legged lurch minus the other two legs.

By the time I reach the yard, the front door of the house has been knocked ajar and the portable battering ram is lying abandoned a short distance inside in its doorway. Authoritative yelling is being met by panicked screaming from inside, but I don't hear a single gunshot.

After a few moments, Frank appears in the doorway and motions for me to join him. He doesn't look happy.

"No Jacks?" I ask as I step inside the house to the disturbing sound of babies crying on an upper floor.

Frank shakes his head. "But you were right about this place."

"How many babies?" I ask.

"Eight."

"The mothers?"

"There's a pregnant gal in a room upstairs who looks ready to pop, but no sign of any others."

"Berta?"

Frank shrugs. "Take a look around. I need to call Social Services."

On the main floor, I find two women sitting in the kitchen under the watchful eye of an armed SWAT officer who took down the rear door. Both women are shaken up; apparently they also believed they were working for a legit organization. One of them is a cook, the other a cleaner.

"Do you know the reverend?" I ask.

"Yes, of course," says the cook.

"Has he been here today?"

"I haven't seen him."

"When did you start work?"

"Less than an hour ago."

I turn to the cleaner. "What about you?"

"We arrived together, same as every day."

Upstairs, I talk with a doula who is looking after the pregnant woman. I ask her the same question.

"Yes," she answers. "The reverend was here."

"Did he have anyone with him? A young woman."

The doula nods and touches the side of her face. "The woman with scars."

My heart leaps. "Yes. You saw her?"

"Only briefly. The reverend was in a rush."

"Do you know where they were going?"

"He didn't say."

"When did he leave?"

The doula shrugs. "I'm not sure. I only came out of the room when I heard someone in the house. When I saw it was the reverend, I came back in here."

"Does he have an office?"

"Yes, next to the nursery."

Before entering the office, I pop my head into the nursery to see Detective Shaw talking with a young woman while she tries to comfort eight crying babies. She's placed one of the calmer ones in his arms, and when he spots me, he offers a smile. Instead of being laced with scorn, it actually appears genuine.

Puzzled, I return the gesture before retreating.

In the hall, Frank arrives at the top of the stairs to tell me Social Services is on its way.

"Jacks was here," I tell him. "With Berta. The doula saw them but doesn't know where they went." I point at the open door beside the nursery. "That's his office. He's pretending to be a reverend."

Inside, one of the SWAT guys is operating a strange machine that looks a bit like a hand-held vacuum cleaner.

"What you got?" asks Frank.

"Explosive signature," says the officer. "Something's been stored here recently."

He places the device on the ground in front of a metal cabinet and starts to ease open the door.

"Wait!" I say aloud. "Is this safe? He had a tripwire at his last place and there's a nursery right next door."

"Signal is minimal," says the officer. "If there were explosives here, they've been removed."

"You hope," I add. "You're talking about someone who stores explosives directly beside a nursery filled with newborns."

The officer shrugs. "C-4 is actually quite stable in its regular form. It takes a considerable shock to set off the chemical reaction of the RDX. Even a gunshot won't do it. That's why you need a detonator."

"Fascinating," I say dryly. "You must be wonderful at parties."

Frank suppresses a smirk as the officer returns to the task at hand and opens the cabinet. From inside, he removes a round, silicone hump with white straps. When he turns it toward me, I see that it's an incredibly detailed fake belly complete with popped belly button. It's so lifelike, I can actually see purple stretch marks in the silicone skin.

Laying it on the floor, the officer finds a velcro seam on the back that allows entry to the belly's hollow interior. The hollow is empty.

Not realizing I have been holding my breath, I exhale in relief before taking a closer look at the cabinet. Despite its wardrobe size, it's empty except for two plain black shirts and a lone pair of black pants. Neither shirt has a standard collar.

"There's room in there for a second prosthetic," I say. "What if the explosives were inside that one? Would that register on your machine?"

The officer nods. "That could give me this reading."

"Shit! What if that's why he took Berta? He's making her wear the pregnancy belly stuffed with explosives."

"But why?" asks Frank. "His operation is finished. We've shut it down."

"But he still needs to get out of town," I argue. "If he's been smuggling money out of the country, it doesn't do him any good unless he can join it."

"So how does a bomb solve that?"

"He's sticking to his original plan. You said it earlier—with Homeland Security involved, you have to take any threat seriously. A bomb in a hospital will bring every agency running, leaving the airports free and clear, especially for a man of the cloth traveling alone." I point at the shirts. "He must have a clerical collar on him and some form of fake church ID."

"But he uses a remote detonator, which means he has to be near the bomb."

"No, he doesn't," I argue. "All he has to do is convince Berta that he's nearby and she'll cause all the panic he needs. He's already killed one woman, so the threat is just as effective as another explosion."

"It's twisted," says Frank, "but I can't argue the logic."

"One problem," interrupts the officer.

"What's that?" I ask.

"How do we know what hospital he's going to target? We don't have enough bomb techs to cover them all and we can't take the risk that it's only a threat."

Frank looks at me and says, "St. Luke's?"

I wince. "I'm not sure. I still think that was a distraction for something else. When he told me to give you that tip, he wasn't expecting his operation to fall apart. He was planning to stick around." I pause. "What if he wanted you at St. Luke's while he detonated a bomb somewhere else?"

"Why?"

I tell Frank what Jacks told me about wanting to create a demand for his surplus of babies.

"That's fucked up," says the SWAT officer.

"But he's capable of it," I add. "We've seen that."

"So we're back to square one," says Frank.

"Not necessarily." I recall what the woman in blue told me earlier. "He has an arrangement with a hospital. Maybe he pays a doctor or nurse for emergency access when things go wrong here. I saw Ania's scar. Whoever is performing the c-sections isn't very skilled, so it's somebody below a surgeon but with access to a little knowledge and the right equipment."

Frank looks over his shoulder and nods. "Let's talk to the doula."

TWENTY-FIVE

THE MANHUNT FOR ELDRED Jacks quickly becomes a nightmare of city-wide logistics and inter-department cooperation that sees me quickly pushed out of the picture.

"You're a civilian," Frank tells me. "You can't be involved."

"Too late," I argue. "I already am."

"Not anymore. Go back to your newsroom and let me do my job. When we catch him, you'll be my first call."

Deposited on the other side of the police tape, I'm instantly engulfed by my fellow media brothers and sisters demanding to know what is going on. They quickly lose interest when I tell them I haven't a clue.

As I drift toward the far edge of the crowd, the young *NOW* reporter, John Underwood, sidles up beside me.

"How do you always gain access to the good side of the yellow tape?" he asks.

"The trick," I answer, "is to get there before the tape goes up."

"And how do you do that?"

"By thinking differently from everyone else." I indicate the media mob. "They've been told their job is to follow a story and cover it better than the competition. None of them ever actually think about *breaking* a story because that means taking a risk that has as good a chance of failure than success. That's why they'll always be on this side of the tape."

"And you're a risk taker?" asks John.

"No." I smile. "I'm far more dangerous than that. I'm the girl your mother warned you about. The stick of dynamite that dances in the flames and gives her editor palpitations. I'm the dinosaur who knows the meteor is coming, but would rather stand and fight than run."

"I don't get it," says the young man.

"You will," I reassure him. "One day."

As I walk away, leaving John looking baffled, I dig out my phone and call Dr. Irena Krawiec.

"Our guest get away okay?" I ask.

"*Tak.*"

"She going to cause you any trouble?"

"I do not believe so. I explain what her reverend has been doing with girls and babies. She is truly horrified."

"Good."

"What is happening there?"

"Shit. Fan. You know? But I'm wondering if you have a photo of Berta."

"No, but Julita is always taking photos with her phone. She may have one."

"Do you have her number?"

"*Tak.* Hold on."

227

When I enter the newsroom, Stoogan makes a beeline for my desk from the opposite side of the room so that we both arrive at the same time.

"Do you have any idea what's going on out there?" he asks breathlessly. "And what the hell happened to your face?"

"I should be insulted that your concern for my well-being comes second to your concern about the news, but I'll let it slide."

"You evaded both questions."

"Pretty tricky, huh?"

"Spill."

"There's a mad bomber out there, but he's not the story."

"Everyone else says he is."

"Exactly."

Stoogan sighs and scratches at his nose. "So what is the story?"

I show him my phone, which he has to pluck out of my hand in order to hold it close enough to his face to see the photo displayed on its screen.

"Who's she?" he asks.

"The real story."

Stoogan hands me back my phone.

"Everyone's looking for the bomber," I continue, "but she's the one we need to find. And we need to find her fast."

"Write it," says Stoogan. "We can go live on the web as soon as you're done."

I grin. "Maybe there is something to this online journalism after all."

"God help us all," Stoogan mutters as he plods away.

TWENTY-SIX

WITH BERTA'S STORY LIVE on *NOW*'s website, accompanied by a photo and a plea for any sightings to be reported to the newsdesk, I climb into a taxi and play the only hunch I have. The doula said Jacks had an arrangement with somebody at a campus of the California Pacific Medical Center, in Presidio Heights. She didn't have many details, but her awkward evasiveness made it clear she was fully aware it wasn't legit.

When I asked about the amateur quality of the women's cesarian scars, she stopped being cooperative and requested a lawyer. Frank asked me to leave the room when I lost my temper and attempted to show the woman where she could stick her request.

Two police cars, lights blazing but sirens on mute, speed past us as we cross Presidio Avenue on California Street. They screech to a halt a short distance ahead, blocking the entire street.

"Go right," I order the cab driver. "Sacramento might still be open."

I wonder if Frank has ordered a cordon around all the hospitals or if he's playing the same hunch and gambling on California Pacific's Women and Children's Center and St. Luke's being the two most obvious targets. Regardless, neither hospital can possibly have enough ambulances on hand for a full-scale evacuation. If Berta is inside, it may already be too late.

The driver makes a sharp turn onto Walnut, followed by a sharper left on Sacramento. As he does, I spot more flashing lights rushing up behind us.

"Floor it," I tell him. "They're not worried about speeding tickets today."

We slip past Spruce Street seconds before the two squad cars block the road behind us. More red and blue lights appear ahead and off to both sides.

"Drop me here," I say.

"What do I say to the police?" asks the driver nervously. "They'll ask what I'm doing here before letting me pass."

"Tell the truth, just don't mention my name. Which is easy, since you don't know it."

"So not all the truth?"

"You dropped off a gorgeous redhead, what more is there to say?"

"So I lie?"

"That just cost you your tip."

He opens his mouth to protest, but my glare tells him he's better off staying quiet.

Dixie's Tips #29: *Married men are always easier to control with a look, as they've already been taught they're wrong 99 per-*

cent of the time. The longer the marriage, the easier they buckle. It's the single ones that still need to be broken.

I slip out of the taxi and turn up the collar of my leather bomber against an icy, foreboding wind before making my way to the rear of the sprawling hospital. It's like I told John earlier: it's far easier to get behind police lines before they erect their barriers in the first place.

As I near the Sacramento Street entrance, two police cars converge in a V shape and park. I turn away before they see my face in case they're under orders to keep the press away.

Making my way around the edge of the building, I look for the tell-tale signs of cigarette butts. I find a collection of old coffee cans filled with rain water and sand outside a fire exit about a third of the way around the side. The doorway has a short overhang that allows smokers to fill their lungs with some shelter from the weather, and the lack of any nearby windows means nobody is disturbed by wafting clouds of second-hand smoke.

The door is locked when I try it, but a cursory examination of the fresh butts tells me I won't have to wait long. Even a police lockdown can't keep an addict from his or her fix.

The frigid wind is a harbinger of an approaching storm and the clouds churning overhead grow darker by the second. I zip my coat against the chill and bend down to pick up one of the larger butt-ends: a half-smoked Camel with a pungent odor. I hold it between my fingers and wait.

When the door opens for a trio of nurses, cigarettes and lighters at the ready, I make a display of crushing the dead cigarette into the sand and offering up a smile.

"No rest for the wicked," I say, grabbing the door before it closes.

"Amen to that, sister," says one of the nurses with a laugh as she lights up.

Her two friends join in with a chuckle and flick their disposable lighters as I disappear inside.

Having entered the bowels of the hospital beneath the patient areas, I'm amazed at the complexity of the working maze. This is where the hidden world exists—a human ant farm of food services, janitorial, and laundry; supply warehouse of bandages, catheters, needles, and body bags; medical waste disposal, including severed limbs and diseased internal organs; the morgue; and who knows what else.

Dr. Frankenstein would likely feel he had been dropped into a secret toy shop filled with medical wonders, while I imagine a horned Minotaur is going to charge around the corner at any moment with hate-filled eyes and a bloodthirst for any and all intruders.

An elevator pings ahead with the promise of escape and I make a dash for it, sliding to a halt on the slick floor before slamming into an exiting gurney being pushed by a balding man in blue hospital scrubs and glaring pink sneakers. The gurney contains the sheeted shape of a patient who is no longer in need of a bed, but in desperate need of a hose nozzle.

"Alfred," the attendant says.

"Dixie," I answer automatically.

The man grins, showing a broken set of twisted teeth. "*He's* Alfred," the man says. "From the top floor?"

"Ahh," I say as if I should have known. "Shame."

"Shame?" The man laughs again. "You must be new. This nasty ol' bugger made everyone's life a misery. The nurses'll be having a party later, you mark my words."

"Right."

He wipes his right hand on his trouser leg and holds it out. "I'm Tobias. When did you start?"

Despite feeling slightly queasy that he had to wipe his hand first, I shake the offered flesh.

"First day," I lie. "Still filling out all the paperwork."

"Yeah, lots of that. Well, careful you don't get lost. It happens to most newbies at least once, 'specially down here."

I point to the elevator. "I was just going to head up. Is that OK?"

"I don't think Alfred will object, which makes it a first for him."

He laughs at his own joke and appreciates it when I join in.

Before stepping into the elevator, the hairs on the back of my neck twitch, and I suddenly blurt, "Do you know Reverend Jacks?"

Tobias's face compresses in thought before he shakes his large head. "Nope. He new, too?"

"Must be."

I enter the elevator and head up to the main floor.

Back in the world of polished floors, clean walls, and the illusion of order, I search out the maternity ward. With more than six thousand births per year in nearly sixty labor/delivery/recovery/postpartum rooms, the Women and Children's Center at the hospital is one of the busiest in the city.

Before I reach the Newborn Connections area, I'm cut off by the arrival of more police officers who station themselves at the lobby entrance. If Berta isn't already inside, Jacks is going to be forced to come up with another plan. But so far, he's always been one step ahead.

Deciding to risk being thrown out of the hospital and beyond the crime scene tape, I walk up to the officers guarding the lobby entrance to Newborn Connections. I unzip my coat so they can see I'm not sporting a pregnant belly, and offer a friendly smile.

"Anything wrong, officers?" I ask. "My sister's in there."

The young patrolman shakes his head. "Just routine, ma'am. Nothing to worry about."

"Can I go in?"

The young man scans me from head to toe, but there's no hint of recognition, which is both a relief and slightly irritating. Don't young men read anymore?

He lets me pass.

Inside Newborn Connections, I pull out my phone and show the photo of Berta to the secretary.

"Has this woman checked in today?" I ask.

The woman studies the photo closely. "Doesn't look familiar. I would remember those scars. Poor girl. Is she registered with us?"

"She wouldn't be registered, but it could have been an emergency."

"Let me check the computer." She types on her keyboard for a moment, clicks her mouse several times and types some more. "Nope. No emergency admittance in Maternity so far today. Sorry. Is she a relative?"

"Yes. Younger sister, two days past due and she's not answering her phone. If there was an emergency, or if she came in by ambulance, where would she be admitted?"

"Emergency, next door, but we would be notified immediately."

I thank her and return to the lobby. Maybe my hunch is wrong, or Jacks saw the cops and decided it wasn't worth the risk.

I find Emergency and study the group of injured and sickly folks awaiting admittance. None of them are Berta. I turn and head back toward the cafeteria, contemplating what Jacks would have done.

Poor, sweet Berta knows exactly what this monster is capable of. She knew all about Ania and how he had detonated the bomb inside her. The moment he strapped that fake belly onto her, she would know her life was over. Jacks isn't a man to bluff, but he also picked the wrong woman.

Berta has already been through so much in her young life. Like Ania, she isn't about to let some prick of a man decide her fate. She wouldn't blindly do what he asked because of some promise that things would be worse if she didn't. Berta already knew worse. She had lived worse and survived, and now with her ragtag band of pissed-off Polish vigilantes she was fighting to free other women from the same slavery she was forced into.

If anything, she would have spit in Jacks's eye and told him to take a flying leap.

The thought stops me in my tracks and I look up at the ceiling.

Like Ania before her, would Berta have climbed to the highest peak? With her fate already sealed, would she take the blast away from as many innocent people as possible?

A smile crosses my lips as the thought solidifies: *Of course she would. My brave, brave girl.*

I rush to the elevator.

———

The elevator releases me onto a quiet floor that smells of death barely kept at bay and too much industrial, germ-killing cleaner. The patients on this floor are moved here for one reason: it's out of the way. The next step is being wheeled to the elevator and down to the basement by an orderly with a crooked smile and pink sneakers.

I find the stairwell and head to the roof.

At the top of the stairs, the red metal door has a large sign bolted to it that warns a fire alarm will sound if the door is breeched. I hesitate for just a moment before pressing the bar and stepping outside.

No alarm sounds.

Standing on the tar and gravel rooftop, I shudder from the wind that pierces my short jacket and coats my tongue with the taste of smog and sea salt. I miss my longer green coat. I listen for the sounds of movement, but the approaching storm whistles in my ears instead.

The flat, irregular-shaped roof is sprinkled with an assortment of large shapes in metal, brick, and wood that house and protect air-conditioning units, ventilation and elevator shafts, radio and television transmitters, emergency generators, and other things I don't recognize. Some of the objects are as large as garden sheds, others more like shiny chrome toadstools in a robotic *Alice in Wonderland* adventure.

As the cold quickly numbs my nose and ears, makes my eyes water, and my fingers stiff, I choose a direction to explore. If Berta did climb up here, she would want to go to the least populated part of the hospital—not an easy task considering the complex is surrounded on all sides by busy streets and businesses. Except, I reason, one corner opens onto a postage-stamp park with a few tall trees that have managed to survive the concrete invasion of urban progress.

On a sunny day that park would be full of people—both patients and visitors—trying to pretend they were somewhere else, but the biting wind of the storm will have chased everyone back inside.

I move toward that corner of the building at a half-run, and as I break past a small brick building that houses another elevator shaft, I see her.

Berta is standing on the edge of the building, staring down at the small park.

I call her name, but the wind carries it away before the sound can reach her.

I yell louder as I narrow the gap until she finally turns around.

The young girl I had known has vanished from her eyes and her pale flesh is so blue from the cold, she barely looks alive. Beneath a man's baggy coat, her stomach bulges. When she recognizes me, she holds up a hand to stop my approach.

"It's OK," I yell to be heard. "He's bluffing."

Berta shakes her head.

"He is," I call back. "He's using you as a distraction so that he can escape the country. We can disarm it."

Berta shakes her head even more rigorously, and I wonder if Jacks has tricked us and rigged up a timer.

"I try to remove," she says. "But it is locked on."

"Let me see."

I walk forward again despite Berta's growing agitation.

"Take off your coat," I say. "I can help."

Tears fall from Berta's eyes, but the bitter wind snatches them from her cheeks before they have time to leave tracks. She drops her coat to the ground and exposes the silicone belly in all its disturbing detail.

I close the gap until I'm inches away.

"You should not have come," she says. "He is not a bluffing man."

"He is," I insist. "We've broken his organization. He'll be rushing to the airport right now, trying to escape."

"No. He is here."

"He brought you here?" I clarify.

"Yes."

"But he's not here now."

"He is."

"I don't see him."

"I ran away when I saw where he was taking me. He wanted me to go where babies are born. How can someone be so cruel?"

"I don't know, but he wouldn't have stayed." I reach over the fake baby bump and touch my cold cheek to hers. "You brave, brave girl. You defeated him."

"I do not think so." Her voice is as dead as her eyes. "He was too angry to run away. I have seen this before in men. They stop thinking and lash out with fists and feet. He has a bomb. He wants to use it."

"We won't let him."

I pull away to reach for my phone and call Frank, but in that moment Berta gasps and her eyes widen at something, someone, who has appeared on the rooftop behind me.

My hunch was wrong. Jacks isn't bluffing.

Instead of turning around, I immediately slip behind Berta, using her as a shield. I whisper in her ear to remain calm as over her shoulder I watch Jacks, dressed in his clerical outfit, moving swiftly across the roof toward us. He's aiming a gun with one hand while holding a remote detonator in the other.

"Dixie Flynn!" he yells through clenched teeth as he narrows the gap. "Hiding behind a pregnant woman?"

"Better a coward than being shot in the back," I yell back.

Jacks's laugh has a nasty, razor-sharp edge. "True. You moved before I was ready. I wanted you down and squirming for the big event."

"You're the one out of moves, Jacks. The police have the hospital cordoned off. They know your plan. You're finished."

He holds up the remote detonator. "I still have you two."

"Not much of a statement compared to a maternity ward."

"But good enough to allow a man of the cloth to escape in the confusion. Who would stop me?"

"Everyone. The police know all about your disguise. They shut down your baby factory this morning and arrested a woman smuggling your money out of the country in her fake womb. At this exact moment, they're tracing every cent you ever squirreled away. You brought Homeland Security into this, and they have the jurisdiction to wipe you out. You should have fled when you had the chance."

Jacks comes to a halt about fifteen feet away and aims his gun at Berta's chest. His face has lost some of its bravado and a nervous twitch is making his lips quiver.

"I shoot her and you have nothing to hide behind. I don't need her alive to explode."

I show him a flash of steel from my pearl-handled switchblade. "I won't go easy."

Jacks laughs again. "Trust a girl to bring a knife to a bomb fight."

"It doesn't have to be this way. You leave the detonator on the ground and I'll call the police to disarm the bomb. I won't tell them you were here until Berta's safe. You'll get a head start."

"And where will I go? You just said they know all about my money. Without that, I have nothing."

"I doubt that," I call back, using the same psychology that every woman knows about a man. When in doubt, stroke his ego. "You're far too clever to put everything in one bank. I'm sure you've got enough to go sit on a beach in Belize for awhile and ponder your future. But you trigger this bomb and you'll never rest. You'll be looking over your shoulder for the rest of your very short life."

"You think damn highly of yourself."

"Not of me, but my friends. The same one who came to my rescue in your building will hunt you down. He doesn't give a damn about extradition treaties or international borders. His only concern will be making you suffer and scream."

Jacks's gaze locks onto mine and in that frozen instant of doubt, I whisper in Berta's ear again before grabbing the top of her head and shoving her roughly to the ground. The bomb-laden belly stays in place as I grip the knife-slashed straps and rush forward like a fearless Spartan warrior, leaping over Berta's prone form.

Jacks staggers backward in surprise as I sprint toward him at full speed, the silicone belly held high as my only shield. It only takes a fraction of a second for him to realize what I've done; the real reason I slid behind my friend and unsheathed my knife.

And in that moment of clarity, he regains some of his composure and brings his gun to bear. It's his only move. With every step, I bring the lethal bomb closer to him.

The impact of the first bullet into the belly fills me with terror as I pray the SWAT officer knew what he was talking about back at the baby factory. Despite everything he said about the relative stability of C-4 plastic explosives, the thought of them not detonating when *shot* seems a near impossibility.

Fortunately, the science holds true as Jacks continues to riddle the belly with bullets, hoping to break through the silicone and plastique shield to puncture flesh as I quickly close the gap between us.

When I slam into him, we're both surprised. But as we tumble to the ground, I have one more task to complete. Ignoring the gun in his right hand, I slam my knife deep into his left hand, piercing the flesh completely and pinning it the roof.

Jacks screams in pain as I scramble off the backside of the fake belly and find my feet.

"You fucking bitch!" he screams. "I'll kill you."

Leaving him to his rage, and without a single snappy comeback, I turn and run away with every ounce of strength I have left.

Stitches rip in my wounded leg and my lungs burn from the effort as I sprint across the roof toward my intended destination. Knowing I'm exposed, my ears prick alert when Jacks's gun erupts with one final bullet before his clip runs dry. I wince in alarm as the bullet zips under my arm, tearing a small hole in the armpit of my jacket, before knocking the cap off one of the metal mushrooms that litter the roof.

"Dixie!" Berta screams from behind the brick-enclosed elevator shaft where I had told her to run. She seems so close and yet still so far as I beg my clumsy feet not to trip, *not yet, not now.*

When I'm near enough, I grab Berta's outstretched hand and siphon some of her strength to dive behind the small brick building in a spray of tar and gravel.

Jacks is still screaming for blood as he struggles to unpin the knife from his hand. Behind the bricks, I unclasp my own hand to show Berta the object I snatched from Jacks's damaged grasp before fleeing: the remote detonator. She nods once in agreement before, barely able to breathe, I flick the switch to turn it on.

Before I can hesitate, Berta closes her hand over mine and together we press the button.

For Ania.

The resulting explosion deafens us.

TWENTY-SEVEN

"JESUS H. CHRIST, DIX!" Frank yells when he finally appears on the rooftop. "How in hell's damnation did you get up here?"

"A hunch," I say.

Berta and I are sitting on the roof with our backs against the brick elevator shaft, although we've moved around to face the carnage rather then being protected from it. Facing this way, the building is sheltering us again, but this time from the wind. Shocked hospital staffers handed us blankets to keep us warm, but the first officers on the scene warned us not to even think about leaving.

I continue. "Ania went to the roof of that parking garage when she didn't know where else to go. I figured Berta might do the same."

"And I did," says Berta.

"She's a hero," I say.

Frank turns to look over his shoulder, where a large hole in the roof is being examined by both police Forensics and structural engineers. Apart from a few fallen tiles and a broken water pipe, nobody inside the hospital was injured.

"And that's Jacks?" he asks.

"What's left of him."

"Care to explain?"

"We got lucky."

"I need more than that."

I fix him with a cold stare. "I cut the bomb off Berta and we made a run for it. If Jacks had detonated it a moment earlier, you would be scraping three bodies off the roof."

"And it's a miracle I'm not," he snaps. "How many times are you going to take these risks? The moment you saw Berta, you should have called me."

"There was no time."

Frank's eyes harden into stone. "You can't rely on luck, Dix. This is life and death you're dealing with."

"Exactly," I snarl. "And we're alive!"

We're interrupted by the coroner, Ruth, who approaches us with a plastic evidence bag clutched in her hand. Inside is the gory stump of a hairy wrist and a bloody hand gripping the smashed components of a remote trigger.

I just hope nobody examines the hand too closely and wonders what caused the palm to be pierced straight through. The knife that held it in place to the roof while the rest of Jacks's body was blowin' in the wind has since been returned to its sheath in my boot.

"It's Eldred Jacks," Ruth says with a delighted chirp. "Convenient of him to leave his hand behind. Not much else survived the blast."

"How can you be sure it's him?" Frank asks grumpily.

Ruth beams and digs out her smartphone. "I have a new app that connects with our database. I've already run his fingerprints. They're a match for those Scotland Yard sent over earlier."

"Cool," I say. "Can I get that on my phone?"

Frank snorts. "What the hell for?"

"Hey, it's tough out there on the dating scene. Be nice to run a criminal check before I've invested a lot of time, you know?"

Ruth laughs. "Good idea."

"No," says Frank, his mood unimproved. "Police work stays with the police."

"Oh, don't be so pissy, Frank. It was a joke. We survived; Jacks didn't. Be happy."

"Be happy? Everywhere you go, people turn up dead."

"*Bad* people."

"For now."

"What does that mean?"

"It means you take too many damn chances and one of these days a lot of people are going to get hurt."

"But not today," I challenge back. "Today, Berta is safe and that scumbag Jacks is dead. So lighten the fuck up."

With a scowl on his face, Frank turns heel and stomps away to examine the hole in the roof. After he's gone, Ruth squats down beside Berta and me, the plastic-wrapped hand resting in her lap as though it's a bouquet of flowers or fresh shoulder of lamb.

"He's just worried about you," she says in a gentle, albeit motherly, tone. "He's come to think of you as the daughter he never had. If he could, he would wrap you in cotton wool and never let you out of his sight."

"Well he could show it better," I say, my voice breaking slightly under stress. "Instead of yelling at me because I survived, a hug wouldn't go amiss."

Ruth smiles. "I'm sure that's exactly what he wants to do, but in front of his officers he has to be the snarly old bear."

Berta reaches out to squeeze my hand. "I see love in his eyes with every word. You are lucky to have such a good man looking out for you."

I squeeze her hand back, acknowledging the wisdom of her words.

TWENTY-EIGHT

RETURNING HOME IN THE dark after finally being released by both the police and an emergency-room doctor, I stop in the lobby and retrieve the last red package from my mailbox. It's larger than the others; heavier and more ominous.

I unwrap it as I climb the stairs, crumpling the paper in my hand and absently dropping it to the ground without thought for neighbors or friends.

Outside my apartment door, I lift the lid on the box and retrieve its contents: a small doll with bright orange hair and a green coat. Wrapped tight around the doll's neck is a twisted length of rope with a short tail ending in a brass eyelet meant for the matching hook on the gallows.

Sighing heavily, I enter the apartment and hang the doll from the miniature gallows. The final tile also slips into place, completing the spelling of my name.

There is no other note, but the threat is clear.

Somebody wants me dead.

Someone other than the man I just blew to pieces on the rooftop of a hospital.

Prince Marmalade bumps his head against my stitched-up leg and purrs loudly when I bend down to scratch his chin. His purr grows even louder when I fill up his food dish.

Too wired to sleep, I reach into the cupboard and retrieve a bottle of cognac that Mr. French recommended for the budget-conscious consumer. Along with a single crystal snifter, I also remove a cigar and lighter from a drawer by the stove and head back downstairs.

Sitting on the front step, I pour cognac into the glass. The storm has passed. The night air is crisp, fresh, and eerily quiet. After the first sip of cognac, I prepare the cigar and touch flame to tip. The fragrant smoke glides over my tongue and around my mouth like a playful lover before finding its escape over my lips again.

The cognac is sweet fire, meant to be savored. It warms my insides and quiets the *thud, thud, thudding* inside my skull.

A car door opens a short distance away and a man steps out. He walks towards me with focused attention, but I don't leave my perch.

Let him come, I tell myself. *I won't be afraid of shadows.*

When he reaches the base of the stairs, he tilts his chin skyward toward the porch light so that I can clearly see his face.

"Detective Shaw," I say, hiding my surprise. "Care to join me for a drink?"

He shakes his head, but offers up a smile. "I just wanted to say sorry."

"Sorry?"

"You're a bull in a china shop," he says. "You're reckless, impulsive, and downright dangerous. But—"

"I'm glad there's a but," I interrupt. "Otherwise you're just ruining the whole sorry part."

He smiles nervously. "I've been acting like a dick. I think I was jealous. The way Frank looks up to you. He seems to pay more attention to whatever you have to say than anything I do, and . . . well, it bothered me."

"What's changed your mind?" I ask, exhaling a cloud of Cuban smoke.

"The babies," he says. "If you weren't as pigheaded as you are, we might never have found that place. Elna told me how many babies she's taken care of. The number of women who had been through there, who had their babies taken away and sold to strangers."

"Elna?"

He smiles again, but warmer this time. "In the nursery. She was looking after the babies."

"Ah." I remember back, trying to bring up her face. Young, pretty, child-bearing hips. A good match for a young detective with a bright future ahead.

"Anyways." He looks down and twists the toe of his shoe into the concrete step. "I just wanted to say that I might have misjudged you."

Now it's my time to shake my head. "You didn't." I think of the doll hanging from a noose upstairs. "I am reckless, but every now and again, I get lucky." I lift my glass. "Sure you don't want a drink?"

"No thanks, I need to get ba—"

The sound of a slamming car door stops Shaw in mid-sentence, and we both turn to see a large man rushing across the street toward us with a gun in his left hand. His eyes are blazing with hatred and in the millisecond between confusion and fear, recognition dawns.

His name is Serge, a Russian hitman who vowed to kill me for destroying his livelihood after Pinch shot off his trigger finger. He'd been working for Krasnyi Lebed at the time. The first time he tried to collect, I left him for dead in an autowrecker's yard. I hadn't thought much of him since, but obviously the same wasn't true of him.

The first bullet slams into the front door mere inches from my head as I scramble down the steps. The second bullet kicks up slivers of concrete that spatter my cheek and left eye. Half-blind, I don't know in which direction to turn when Shaw flattens me to the ground and yells, "Stay down!"

The young detective clears his gun from his holster, but he's missing the one ingredient that makes a professional hitman so dangerous: total lack of fear.

Shaw's first shot would have made his instructors proud. It hits the Russian center-mass. Unfortunately, unlike the shooting range, it only knocks the assassin back half a step before he continues his charge.

I scream as Shaw and the assassin trade bullets before Serge's left hand becomes as deadly as his right used to be and a bullet smashes into Shaw's skull. The young detective's gun hand falls limp and his warm blood flows over me as I lay on the steps, my legs trapped beneath his weight.

"This is last chance," says Serge as he arrives at the bottom of the steps and aims his gun at my head. "No more game. Hangman is over. I want to know who took my finger."

I had never told him that it was Pinch. Not that it matters. I can see in his eyes he doesn't intend for me to live.

"Fuck your finger," I say.

"Say goodbye."

A small crimson dot suddenly darts across his eye and centers on his forehead, staying his hand. He glances skyward toward my apartment and I take the only chance I have left. Reaching forward to grasp Shaw's limp hand, I slip my trigger finger over his and bring his gun to bear.

The assassin quickly turns his attention back to me, but I'm already squeezing the trigger and I have no intention of stopping.

From this low angle, every shot enters his chest from below, tearing apart his insides like a water balloon dropped on a bed of nails.

He's dead before the realization dims the fury in his eyes.

When the gun runs dry and the assassin crumples to the sidewalk, I drop Shaw's hand and glance up toward my window. A young blonde mother-to-be is standing there with my gun in her hand, her finger squeezing the button of its laser sight. She looks horrified and scared and like the most beautiful angel I have ever seen.

Cradling Shaw in my arms, I yell for someone to call for an ambulance. I know it's too late, but I keep yelling until someone squeezes my shoulder and says it's okay to let go.

I don't dare.

I can't.

In the distance, sirens sound.

THE END

© Don Denton, Black Press

ABOUT THE AUTHOR

M.C. Grant is the secret identity of international thriller writer Grant McKenzie. (Oops, there goes that secret.) Born in Scotland, living in Canada, and writing fast-paced fiction, Grant likes to wear a kilt and toque with his six-guns. Often compared to Harlan Coben and Linwood Barclay, Grant has three internationally published thrillers to his name—*Switch*, *No Cry for Help*, and *K.A.R.M.A.*—that have earned him an avalanche of positive reviews and loyal readership around the globe. As a journalist, he has won numerous awards across Canada and the United States, including one in 2012 from the Association of Alternative Newsmedia—the same organization that Dixie's fictitious *San Francisco NOW* belongs to. He is currently Director of Communications for Our Place Society in Victoria, B.C. You can find him online at http://grantmckenzie.net.

ACKNOWLEDGMENTS

One of the most exciting days in a writer's life is when the product of our imagination is finally in the hands of you, the reader. The reason I write down these adventures (rather than just keep them tumbling around in my head) is to entertain as many people as possible. I may breathe life into Dixie, but it is your support and enjoyment that allows her to flourish. It also takes a team of wonderful, story-loving professionals to make sure my books make it into your hands. To that end, I couldn't ask for a more enthusiastic and generous team than I have found at Midnight Ink.

Word of mouth is also vitally important to a writer, and I value all the support that bookstores, reviewers, and readers have shown to my work. Your love, support, and kindness mean the world to me.

I hope you enjoyed Dixie's third adventure as much as I enjoyed writing it.